Cinderella

A Hero Princess Tale

Fairy Tales for Today Series

Written by Piper Winifred, PhD
Illustrations by Līga Klavīna

ISBN-13:978-1548346720
ISBN-10:1548346721

Table of Contents

Why we Read Fairy Tales

Beyond sheer enjoyment, why do we read fairy tales? As you encounter a Fairy Tale, a Folk Tale, or any Wonder Tale from long ago that has retained its authenticity you will discover something truly amazing: you discover yourself. It never fails, because that is the hallmark of the Wonder Tale. The Journey represented by the story illuminates the path to discovery.

Sometimes truth is difficult to find because it can be elusive, or small, or maybe . . . so big and so wonderful that it cannot be described in simple words. It can be related across the divide between human beings, and over time, through stories about recognizable events and people living out their lives.

What is it like to be a daughter, a mother, a wife, a grandmother, a wise woman, or a fool? What about a merchant, a traveler, a ruler, an adventurer, or a beggar? Stories do not need to preach or explain; they illustrate through vivid characterizations that are universally recognizable.

You may or may not believe in dragons, or ogres like the one Fairer-than-a-Fairy has to face, or believe the monster of a step mother that Cinderella must overcome, but I know that I have encountered unexpected and awful dangers in life for which I was not prepared. Wonder Tales speak to us about how to marshal our resources and use our tools so we will be prepared when the time comes.

You may not tap into nature like the Hero Princess in this tale, but how often have you wished for the proper tools—organic or even magic tools--to complete a seemingly impossible task? Again, I know I have!

Can we and ought we heal others with our gifts? Can we heal ourselves or find refuge from the inevitable storms of life?

When Ella faces these same questions, we ask ourselves about our own lives, and whether and if? Wonder Tales teach us that women derive power through the recognition and utilization of their resources, tools, and skills. Women demonstrate the energy that is power through the use of those same resources, tools, and skills they have learned and acquired on their individual quest.

Fairy tales, folk tales, and wonder tales speak the truth. The truth is, we DO eat poisoned fruit; get lost in the woods; become tongue-tied and at a loss for words, locked in towers or become isolated by bad guys. Sometimes we are placed on pedestals as pretty adornments; or seduced and confused by the Big Bad Wolf. Other times we are reduced to lesser positions and dominated or harmed. Like Cinderella, we do get misunderstood, ignored by those who are supposed to love us, and we are called to find solutions where none seem possible. Then, as now, our sisters: the brave queens, hero princesses, adventurers, women scholars, Old Women, occasional fairies, and even a Lady of the Lake and more have answered the call to step onto The Path and Quest, and we can too!

How to Read a Fairy Tale

How wonderful is it that one of the greatest tools we have available to us has been passed down through the ages in the form of stories . . . many of them by women / for women on a Shared Journey. Time-out-of-mind, women have passed down their knowledge and practical wisdom based on experience and the wealth of shared stories for each other's benefit. Throughout time, women like you and like me have asked themselves the questions you about to encounter on The Path represented by Cinderella's Journey. Hers is complex just as is yours, and just as any woman engaged in living a 21st century life.

Something powerful exists in the knowledge that we belong to a centuries-old community of women who, just like you and me, have asked and answered these same questions. I can draw upon the lore collected in Wonder Tales, which offers real solutions to everyday living both common and profound. Sometimes I find answers to questions I didn't even know I had!

How tragic is it that most Wonder Tales have become so corrupted over the centuries that what we have been given are variations of story cuts and interpretations of stories that no longer hold the original pieces, so they no longer retain the essential elements? They preserve little clues, but together these pieces and clues no longer add up to a meaningful rendering that offers Practical Wisdom as once was the entire purpose of the story!

What happened?

- The authentic versions of women and girls were written out of the epic tales, and the women became sidekicks, or lesser versions of themselves in their own stories.
- Wonder Tales filled with deep meaning evolved into Fairy Tales based on cuteness and fancy descriptions. Mystery and metaphor were replaced by magic and magical creatures. The idea of a "fairy" changed most of all.
- The stories became increasingly geared toward children and thus lost the Journey aspect as they focused on a backwards look to the nursery, instead of a forward look toward Possibility and Potential in a real life.

When you read an authentic Wonder Tale, like this story in the Hero Princess Series, you are reading an authentic tale passed down over the centuries for over 1200 years. The story of Cinderella is also the most common fairy tale in the world, existing in every known culture and land. This story, as with all Wonder Tales, is written NOT for children to READ but to HEAR. This is for teens, young adults, and adult women (And men) with questions and wonderings in their hearts. This is for people who want to think, and seek to understand themselves.

So what about little girls, and especially since we first meet a very young Ella when she is growing up with two loving (if a bit distracted) parents?

The little girls in our worlds: our daughters, sisters, nieces, neighbors, students, and all the little girls who are a part of our lives also want to hear the stories of the great Hero Princesses, and they will. They first need to encounter these stories by hearing them from us in our own words and in our own way, just as stories have ALWAYS been passed down.

As you journey with the Hero Princesses in our Series, and specifically here, with Cinderella and her companions: Alwyn, the birds and Nature along with her mentors: Mildred, Cook, and Nurse you will discover embedded, timeless truths. As already mentioned, the most important truth of all is your own; it is the discovery of your most Authentic Self.

As you tell and re-tell the story to the little girls in your life, you might relate pieces of the story like: "When the Hero Princess learned to cook or weave," or "The day she used her wish, and the birds became a symphony for the household." One of the greatest gifts given to us by Cinderella is her Thinking/Feeling process. She spends a great deal of time processing her emotions, and indeed, she has MUCH to work through. The comparison between her conclusions and the behavior she chooses in contrast to others in the story offers more than just teaching opportunities for little girls, but also reminders for folks in all walks of life.

The pieces of the story are endless and ever-usable for teaching and for THINKING and adapting to our lives; not just for little girls, but for women and men: young and old. And then we pass it on. To help in this process, questions, answers, and notes are included at the end of the story for your enjoyment and use.

Once upon a time . . .[1]

. . . there lived a beautiful maiden named Eleanor, who lived in a bustling little town situated at the edge of a lush, green forest. Her beauty was matched equally by her sweet disposition,[2] and she lived happily with her father and mother in a chateau crowned by seven identical towers rising up from the red poppy fields leading out of town and out into the wider valley[3]. Father spent part of each year at the fairs,[4] and this particular year was especially important for Eleanor, for this year he promised to bring back a special bolt of cloth for her Spring Festival Dress.[5] This year, Eleanor was finally old enough to wear her hair up, and to dance with her friends first in the Maiden's Dance,[6] then dance together with her mother holding a specially woven garland of flowers she would treasure the rest of her life. She thought about the dance, the flowers, the other girls, and the coming excitement with great anticipation.

One drowsy afternoon, strolling through the gardens, Eleanor listened to the bees humming as they worked,[7] and thought about the upcoming festivities.

Growing Up

In previous years, Ella stood at the sidelines during the Maiden's Dance with the other younger girls, clapped her hands listening to the tune played by the fiddle and pipe, tapped her feet in time to the tambourines, and responded with the crowd at the right points in the song. She had watched the older girls move through the steps of the traditional folk dance,[8] but now it would be her turn, and *oh my*-- the day was almost here! Would the fabric Father brought home match the trim she and Mother embroidered as the sunlight faded each evening?

She stood up, and started to pace between the rose bushes as she thought about the upcoming dance. She imagined her skirts floating around her ankles with the evening breeze as she danced. She laughed to herself, thinking of Cook's gentle teasing as she shooed her out of the kitchen with a snap of the dishtowel. She laughed again, imagining Cook's words:

"Aww, go on wit' yer, Miss! Look at ye, all grown up, and still hangin' about the kitchen, babbling about a dance. Surely ye have sometin' ladylike to do wit yer day![9] Go on, now. Be off!"[10]

Despite the scolding, Eleanor knew Cook enjoyed her company. She felt the changes coming into her life, however, and knew things would be different soon. It felt strange. CatStitch, her sweet little cat, jumped up to the bench she had just left, and Eleanor reached down to scratch her behind the ears.[11]

"You feel it too, don't you CatStitch? Things are about to change, and I do not know if I am ready!"[12]

Homecoming

The calico cat meowed loudly, telling her mistress that Father and his men had just turned off the main road and were on the way up the long drive.[13] Tossing away all thoughts of being grown up and ladylike, Eleanor hiked up her skirts and ran towards the main house, flinging open a side door and calling for Mother.

"He is here, Mother! Father is home!"

Mother came to the edge of the gallery at the top of the stairs, radiating excitement despite her attempt at a calm exterior. Issuing orders to Mildred the housekeeper about linens, food arrangements, baths, and a list of other preparations, Mother swept downstairs, grabbed Eleanor's hands in her own, and pushed open the front doors of the Great Hall before Arthur, the footman, could assemble himself.

"Ella, tuck in your hair, dear. Where are your ribbons? Your dress is all-askew. A young lady has a certain appearance to keep."[14]

Mother's smile belied her stern words. Mother and daughter stood at the steps, and keenly watched the horses pull the heavy-laden wagons up the drive and over the bridge, past the gates, and over to the warehouses. Behind them came the soldiers in loose formation, and then finally, Father appeared on Gideon, his favorite stallion. Mother stood on tip-toe, eager to catch a first glimpse of her husband. As he approached, Ella could no longer stand the wait, so she dropped Mother's hand and swiftly ran out to greet him.

Father chided her for her lack of ladylike manners, but laughed anyway. Smiling, he reached into his leather pouch and pulled out long satin ribbons the color of the sky. Dismounting, he placed the ribbons in her hands, and then bowed with great exaggeration.

"Here you are Young Lady. Perhaps these will fit your long, lovely hair…and also remind you of the proper behavior while they're at it!"

Eleanor laughed with delight, wrapping the ribbons around her hair while she simultaneously pretended to dance with an invisible boy. Meanwhile, Father casually handed over his reins while he looked intently at Ella, pretending to act shocked:

"Dancing with boys! Oh no, your mother did not mention this! I cannot countenance my precious daughter dancing with boys!" He kept his eyes on Eleanor, but gestured to Thomas the old handyman and faithful retainer of many years:

"Thomas, come here immediately!" he commanded. "I want you to start building a tower at once. We need to lock this young lady up without delay. She is beginning to think about boys!" Father clutched his heart with one hand and tore off his hat with the other, wrenching his face in a melodramatic grimace.

"Right away, Master!" said Thomas with a grin. Winking at Ella, he turned toward the warehouses, taking Gideon's reins from the footman. "Did yer want me to take care of this beast sire, or will ye be needin' that tower built before supper?"

"Oh the tower, Thomas. Definitely get that tower built immediately. I will tolerate no delays."

"Faaa-ther!" squealed Ella.[15]

Gideon whinnied, and Thomas ambled off, calling ahead to the stable boys, as Father bounded up the front steps and enfolded Mother in his arms. They moved into the Great Hall, whereupon family tradition said the night would be filled with celebration. Fresh rushes redolent of bayberry lined the floor, and dozens of candles burned from three giant chandeliers hanging from the ceiling. Maids stood along the walls, their arms filled with trays piled with honey-dipped fruits, sugared carnations, and meat pies. Footmen stood at attention with silver pitchers filled with spiced wine made from the household's vineyards. Most of all, the house was aglow with anticipation.[16]

"Thank you for the preparations, Mildred," Mother murmured to the housekeeper. "Please thank the other servants for today."

"Yes, Mistress. Thank you," answered Mildred.

Along with Thomas and Cook, Mildred was a mainstay of the household. The delicious food and the delight of Father and the other men having returned warmed everyone's hearts. Once the family retired, the servants continued the festivities, and Eleanor went to sleep, warm and comfortable on her goose down mattress, listening to the music generated from below. Her dreams gave her a sense of satisfaction of all being right with the world.

Tradition

Upon the rising of the sun, Mother and Ella eagerly set to work, laying out the fabric bolts Father had purchased. They began draping them over Ella's shoulders and arms while they waited for Mrs. Henderson, the seamstress, to arrive. Soon enough, Arthur showed the seamstress into the drawing room:

"Mistress, Mrs. Henderson has arrived. Right through here if ye please, Mrs. Henderson," intoned Arthur.

"Thank you Arthur," responded Mother. "Will you fetch Alwyn please?"

"Right away my Lady," responded Arthur, but he jumped when he turned and bumped into Alwyn, the upstairs maid and Ella's frequent attendant, who, unknown to him, stood immediately behind him.

"Ouch!" squealed Alwyn, as Arthur inadvertently stepped on the maid's toes when he turned.

"I'm s-s-ooo sorry," he stammered, flushing a flaming red. "I was just-- I mean I didn't—rather, I meant the Mistress--oh, drat…" he mumbled, and fled back to the entry hall.

Alwyn entered the drawing room smiling, only to find the other women laughing bemusedly, for they had witnessed the entire scene.

"Well, come on girl, let's begin," lectured Mrs. Henderson. "We have a dress to make. No need to be gawking at boys now! You stand right here and do as I say."

"Right away Ma'am," answered Alwyn as she bobbed and moved next to the seamstress.

Alwyn marked the measurements in chalk, sometimes placed stickpins, and dutifully positioned Ella this way and then that, as directed. Ella enjoyed every minute of the process as she tried to imagine the dress from Mother's suggestions and Mrs. Henderson's cryptic remarks and occasional grunts. Finally they were done, and Alwyn followed Mrs. Henderson to the workroom, carrying the folded layers of cloth draped over her arms.

Each evening, Mother and Ella continued to embroider the trim and embellish the strips of beadwork in the old style. This dress represented something more than just the festival, for it embodied generations of tradition. Ella would wear it every year after this as part of her own commemoration of her coming of age, just as Mother and the other women of the town wore theirs to the festival each year, too.

Finally, the day arrived.

Festival Preparations

"Wake up, Miss," called Alwyn, as she entered Eleanor's chambers. "I have a fresh bowl of warm water waiting for ye over at the window. Come on, then. Look out over the flower fields while I wash yer beautiful hair."

Alwyn rinsed and massaged Ella's scalp with her specialty shampoo made of ginger root, birch bark, and white willow moss mixed with honey from the estate's honey combs.[17] She dried Ella's hair by briskly rubbing the long, shiny locks between loving hands covered with a thick, soft cloth: one of many woven by Nurse.[18] CatStitch sat on the bedside table watching, occasionally purring her approval of the fragrant process.

"Now stay right here, Miss, while I refill the bowl with Lavender Rinse to make sure yer hair is nice and shiny for tonight. Don't move now. I'll be right back." Relaxed and happy, Ella nodded her assent, petting CatStitch while she waited for Alwyn to return.

"Here we are now," sung Alwyn when she returned with the steaming bowl of warm Lavender Water mixed with a hint of cider vinegar.

While she rubbed the flower water into Ella's hair, she bade her mistress place her hands in a smaller bowl of Cook's special beauty paste made from pressed olive oil, apricots, and wheat germ.[19]

"Now then, yer hair is more beautiful than it has ever been, and it is indeed that time for ye to lie back and let me press yer face with rose petals and rub those nails. Oh, I'm so happy for ye, Miss!"[20]

Ella asked Alwyn to sit down and talk while they both soaked their hands, and just then, Mother came into the room preceded by the familiar waft of the luscious scent of garden roses that always accompanied her.

"Oh, Sweet Eleanor, my precious daughter. And Allie, too: you are doing a lovely job.

This is such an auspicious day, and a big night for everyone. I hope you and the other girls will have time for your own preparations too?" Ella and Allie looked at each other and smiled. Mother looked out the window and sighed.

"What a lovely thing it is that we can celebrate with flowers from our own garden! I know you love the grounds Ella. You two are both so young. I remember many things that seem a long time ago. I remember when Millie—I mean Mildred-- sat where you now sit, Allie, for once upon a time, she was my ladies maid, did you know that? She came here with me when I married your father, Eleanor.

Mother sighed again. "So many changes! No long thoughts today though, for this is a happy, carefree day!" Mother stood for a moment at the window, looking wistfully out at the horizon, then turned and smiled.[21]

"Tell me please, which hairstyle did you choose for your hair? I know you have been so excited about wearing it up!"

"Oh Mother, you know that Allie and I have been looking at the many portraits in the hall, and practicing the different hairstyles. We are going to surprise you!" answered Ella.

"Oh my," Mother exclaimed. "You can show me tonight, then. I know you will be beautiful. I believe I will rest before the dance." Mother turned to go to her quarters.

Eleanor had enjoyed every part of the festival preparations, but she also worried. Even now at the last minute troubled thoughts whirled through her mind:

"What if no one asks me to dance?" 'What if I forget the steps and movements?" "What if I become embarrassed?"

Gathering at the wishing well with her friends earlier in the week while Mother visited Father's tenants, her friend Alion announced:

"My sister says that everyone knows that whoever asks you to dance for the very first dance is the one you will marry!"

Ella's friend Ginny leaned over close to Ella's ear and whispered, "It's true, I have heard that too!" Something else to be anxious about! What if no one asked her to dance?

As evening approached, the family gathered in the hall and Thomas pulled the carriage around to drive to the village. (The servants would also attend the dance, but amongst themselves and with their own families.)

When Eleanor arrived at the festival, Adela excitedly told her that the boys had already drawn straws for their position to dance with Ella. Did that count as asking she wondered?

Before that time, though, would come the *Maiden's Dance.* Eleanor, along with Alion, Ginny, and Adela formed a circle with the other girls their age, each of them feeling every bit as lovely as they looked in their traditional dresses with ribbons in their hair, holding flower garlands in their hands.

When the fiddler began, accompanied by the 3-string rebek and piper, the girls started with the familiar steps, moving in a circle. They moved around three times, forming an intricate pattern with their feet, reciting the traditional song of spring:

Long, long sunlight-blessed, she opens wide the door;
Now the winter time is past, now the moment to stand fast,
To take the sword within her grasp
... and rule the land once more.

After the first verse, they changed directions and threw their garlands to the center of the ring, then joined hands, and moved in a clockwise direction. As the girls of the town went through the traditional moves, the townspeople sang:

So dance, Maiden, dance -- dance, Maiden, dance!
While the faerie-people sing, traipsing round the maypole ring
The May Queen sets about to bring the world to life with rites of spring --
So dance, Maiden, dance -- dance, Maiden, dance!

Next and by tradition, the mothers of the young women stepped forward, forming a second circle around their daughters.

The young women again changed direction, now moving clockwise, while their mothers moved in counterpoint. They sang in unison.

All throughout the Dark Lord's reign, the Maiden shed the Crone;
In restoring sleep she's lain, gaining strength where once was pain,
She'll be the Mother once again, and come into her own.[22]

There in moonlight stands a stag, then there stands Dark Lord;
Who spies the Bride who once was Hag, garbed in gown that once was rag,
He ascends his thorny crag... to offer and adore.

By this time, the dance was more about stamina than technique alone, but it was important to follow through and keep up with the increased pace. Ella felt as though she danced on air and as if her feet had wings. Never had she been so much in her element. She laughed, and the sound of it rippled through the air like a wave of fairies turning somersaults on the first day of spring. Her eyes sparkled and her teeth gleamed. She felt in tune with the particles of the moonbeams that shone down on the town square. This was a dream come true.

Ella and the other maidens moved to the center and picked up their garlands, raised them high over their heads, and stood in a tight circle. They twirled in place with their garlands raised once, twice, three times, then lowered their arms skipped out to their mothers, who joined with them in holding the beautiful flower garlands. The mother-daughter teams took turns moving over and under raised garland arches, and the mothers of each young girl danced off and out of the circle, each leaving her daughter in place for the finale. The maidens joined hands and sang the refrain:

So dance, Maiden, dance -- dance, Maiden, dance!
While the faerie-people sing, traipsing round the maypole ring
The Queen sets about to bring the world to life with rites of spring –
The Queen of Spring

The townspeople joined together:

So dance, Maiden, dance -- dance, Maiden, dance!

Now the men stood in a line and joined arms, singing as they knelt before the dancing maidens:

Now he kneels before the Queen, and offers her his sword;
Power flows from White to Green, and though she rules the changing scene,
Both will raise the sword between... the Lady and her Lord.

The men stood up and joined the throng, as everyone sang the finale and the young ladies linked arms with their flower garlands entwined.

So dance, Maiden, dance -- dance, Maiden, dance!
While the faerie-people sing, traipsing round the maypole ring
The Queen sets about to bring the world to life with rites of spring –
The Queen of Spring.

So dance, Maiden, dance -- dance, Maiden, dance!
Dance, Maiden, dance -- dance, Maiden, dance! [23]

Once the circle dance drew to a close, the fiddles played for general dancing, and all of Ella's previous worries came for naught, for she was easily the most favored of the maidens as the young men lined up to dance with her. Father looked so proud standing with the other merchants, businessmen, and town leaders, watching and occasionally clapping to the music. Mother's eyes gleamed as she nodded encouragement to her daughter.

At the end of the evening, the Lord Chamberlain sent by the King's orders rose to make a special announcement, and crown one maiden as the *Queen of Spring*. He stood on the platform that had been erected in the middle of the town square, beamed at the crowd, and raised a wreath made of red poppies, yellow buttercups, and daisies high over his head:

On behalf of His Majesty the King,
I am pleased to announce the winner of this year's Spring Festival.
The most beautiful Maiden in the Valley is. . .

He paused dramatically. His eyes swept over the crowd. He sucked in his breath, and exhaled. Then suddenly he announced all at once:

"...and the winner is Eleanor, Queen of Spring!"

Everyone cheered, and in one massive effort pushed her forward.

She blushed and smiled. It all seemed unreal, but also inevitable like a dream; just like the rest of the night. She stepped up onto the platform, and the Lord Chamberlain placed the crown of flowers on her head.[24] He next escorted her back out to the center of the square where Father waited, ready to claim her hand for a dance. Again, people clapped and yelled, and then everyone danced. How proud Father looked, and Mother so flushed. Ella wished this night could last forever. Finally it was time to go home.

"I could not be any happier than I am tonight," she told herself as she tripped up the stairs on her way to her rooms, then dreamily tumbled through her doorway.

She laughed as CatStitch jumped at her skirts, trying to catch the ribbons that flowed from them as she undressed. Her head continued to whirl as she fell into her soft, downy bed.

The clock struck midnight.[25]

Household Knowledge

Time passed in the usual way, and if it were possible, Eleanor grew lovelier with each passing week. Before long, it was time for Father to leave for the fairs once again, and Eleanor continued with her regular household routine.

She especially loved supervising the morning flower arrangements, and often went into the gardens to help select the stems.

Lately Mother had begun leaving the menu preparations to her, and then even delegated to her the weekly meeting with Mildred. Ella loved being in the kitchen, for that meant time to absorb the savory smells of barley and lentil soups along with bread rising, to listen to the chattering of the scullery maids when they thought she was not paying attention to them, and to enjoy the rough but love-filled hugs from Cook-- something she could find nowhere else. She watched the older women who ran the household at her bidding, and learned from studying them how to make and keep a perpetual broth, to sort beans, rinse and soak various grains, peel and chop the vegetables, and to regulate the level of the fires. She learned the names and order of the keys on Mildred's ring, the hierarchy of the staff, the arrangement of the butlery and the buttery, and where and how the cupboards and chests had been ordered. She learned about the seasons from a household viewpoint, and numbers and categories came to mean something new as well.

One afternoon, Ella came in from the rose gardens to find Mildred waiting for her, holding a large basket packed with bread and jars of lentil soup ready to take to the tenants. Mother usually took care of this duty and Ella often went along, but Mildred told her that she would need to go alone, as Mother had not risen that morning.

Tragedy

"I know you warn't plannin' t'go today, dear, but I'm afraid yer Mum has taken to her bed. I've told Allie t' be ready to go along sose t' keep ye company."

Eleanor hurried through her task grateful for Allie's help, and later rushed upstairs to tend to Mother. When she passed into the chamber, she found her dear mother sleeping. Mother did not rise from her bed the next morning, nor the next, and she did not come downstairs. In the days that followed, the only food Mother would take was the soup Ella made under Cook's direction.

Nurse gladly came from her retirement cottage to sit at Mother's bed, coaxing soup and cool liquids down her throat. Mildred and Ella took turns relieving Nurse.

"There, there, now. A little bit more Dear. We've been together a long time now, haven't we Mistress? Now sip some soup for me. There you go," coaxed Nurse.

Mother tried to talk, but she was too weak to finish her thoughts.

"Don't strain yourself trying to talk Mistress, just try and eat something so you can get well," urged Mildred.

"Millie, I want to tell you something important," breathed Mother heavily. "I meant to assign Alwyn as formal ladies maid to Ella, so she will be ready to go with her when she marries, like you did with me."

"Time enough for that, Mistress."

"No, Millie, this is important."

"Hush now, Mistress, I will remember. Stop all this frettin' now," spoke Mildred, and her patient fell fitfully back on her pillow.

After this, Eleanor, Nurse, Mildred, and sometimes Alwyn took turns tending to Mother, sitting by her bedside, placing cool cloths on her brow, coaxing broth down her throat one spoon at a time, propping her up in a chair by the window, and finally, they took turns sleeping in a chair next to her bed. The village doctor came and went to no avail.

Days turned into weeks, and Mother wasted away day by day. They dared not leave her alone, but their efforts seemed pointless nevertheless. Mother's condition seemed to only worsen each day. The doctor dropped in once a week, but offered no different remedy than what they already knew. Meanwhile, Father's trip seemed to last longer than ever before, and Mother continued to weaken before their eyes.

One afternoon after a very long night, Ella sat in the rose garden, thinking about the last few months.

She could not remember when she had last slept or sat down to eat. She ought to be in her rooms catching some much needed rest while she had a moment, but here she sat. She felt restless; probably due to so many hours pent up in the sick room. She sat on her favorite carved bench, hoping the fragrant roses, the warm sun, the bees humming, or maybe the scent of the ripe fruit from the orchards would inspire her; help her think of something to help Mother recover and regain her strength. While she sat in reverie, she realized CatStitch had come to the garden bench to tell her that Father and his men were on the road leading up to the chateau. At last! She stood up and smoothed her dress, recognizing that she looked a sight!

Ella laughed somewhat grimly to herself, thinking: "Well, I suppose I look like someone who has been in the sickroom for countless weeks!"

Did she want to run inside and upstairs to dress like a proper young lady, or did she want to run down the drive and greet her father? What a dilemma! She was no longer a child and knew she was responsible for the family honor, but worry over Mother had taken its toll. She decided to run down the lane immediately. She felt so glad Father had arrived.

She hurried around the side of the east wing, across the sweep of the drive, and over to the bridge, then looked searchingly down the tree-lined path leading up to the chateau.

"Father!"

Eleanor took no notice of the stares from his men as they passed by, leading tired horses and pulling wagons heavy laden with rare textiles from the fairs. Father was just dismissing the guards and giving them last instructions, when he turned and saw her. Immediately a frown formed on his face as he took in her appearance, but she ignored his disapproval.

"Mother is very sick, Father. Hurry! We have been so worried!"

He immediately handed over his reins, and turned to the main house all in one movement. His tall leather boots ate up the ground as he strode up the lane, over the bridge, and into the front entrance, thrusting aside all help and questions as he bounded up the stairs and into the master's chambers.

Death Arrives

What Father saw shocked him. He sat down on the bed and scooped his beloved wife in his arms, suddenly scared, feeling clumsy and overly large when he saw that his touch caused her pain. Nevertheless he could not let her go.

"What ails you my dearest?" he begged of her.

She looked into his face, and smiled wanly. As sick and miserable as she felt, her sweet, calm gaze made him feel better. He saw that her eyes lacked their usual sparkle, and he despaired. Her normally pale white skin appeared almost translucent, and the hollows of her cheeks and under her eyes accentuated her beauty. He felt powerless.

"Fetch the doctor!" he bellowed.

"The doctor has come, but to no use, Father," Eleanor began, but Father was not listening.

"Clear the room," he stated tersely between clenched teeth, so she and the other women quietly tiptoed out.

With Father home, there was much to be done, and Eleanor set about directing the servants to prepare the house. Once things were set in motion, she hurried to her rooms to correct her appearance. All was silent from her parent's chambers. Several hours later, she heard her name summoned to her mother's sick bed. Solemn-faced, Father beckoned her to the door:

"Come in to say good-bye, Eleanor."

Father looked stricken as he turned and left, leaving her alone in the room. She rushed to the bed, sinking next to her Mother, tears flowing.

"Nooo Mother, I cannot bear to lose you! Please do not go. Do not leave me. Not yet."

"Hush, Ella, do not despair," Mother whispered. "I will not be gone, but will always be with you, and will always look over you. Dear One, you have worked so hard taking care of me."

That night, Mother passed into death's arms. All the right prayers were spoken and respects paid, and Eleanor's eyes stayed wet with tears as they laid her beloved Mother into the ground towards the back of the rose garden behind the family estate amongst the dandelions. Only a small marker over the grave indicated her burial place.

Very soon, the whiteness of winter rolled down the mountain and laid its cold bleached blanket over the Earth. Father remained aloof, burying himself in business affairs. He said nothing to Eleanor of the loss they shared, and meanwhile, prosperity and success increased at his slightest touch.

When springtime approached he made ready to travel to the fairs in the north. As he gathered the men and wagons for departure he called his daughter to him:

"Eleanor, you are no longer a child, and I expect things to be handled appropriately while I am gone. I am certain you will live up to expectations." He looked searchingly at her for the first time in months. "Is there anything you wish me to bring back for you?"

Ella thought of the white winter sky, of her starving heart, of death, and of deep loneliness.

She blurted out, "Oh yes, something colorful and bright, please."

For a moment, Father looked at her in the old way, the way he used to look with a bright gleam in his eye, and he almost smiled. His lips parted as he started to answer, but no words came out. He paused.

"Very well then," he said after a thud of a heartbeat and a clearing of his throat.

Eleanor stood on the bridge leading to the family estate and waved good-bye. Normally, a journey lasted four months. She would not see him for almost six.

Ella did not attend that year's Spring Festival, and when Ginny, Alion, Adela and her other friends sent messages, wondering when she would come to town to visit, she put them off, having no heart for their chatter.

Life Goes On

No one in the household noticed the coming of summertime along with the consequent, now former pleasures of heavy fruit hanging from overladen tree limbs, or bees humming dizzily with delight at easy fruit juice. No one cared. Nighttime seemed the same as day, and sleep became difficult to find. Ella began seeking refuge in the garden to sit on her favorite bench in the moonlight as a refuge from sleepless nights. She walked in the garden with the weight of the past months pressing her thoughts into patterns of stillness and quiet, of never ending twilight and halted paths, of sickness and broken dreams.[26]

As she thought, she paced, when suddenly; CatStitch gave notice of Father's return. "In the middle of the night?" Ella asked the cat.

She quickly checked her appearance, mentally went down a checklist regarding the household, and then went outside to wait on the front steps. She saw the usual guards and outriders come up the lane and over the bridge, but then instead of wagons and her Father riding on his large brown steed, a carriage came next, swaying with the weight of baggage, and the coachman attempting to maneuver the turn.

Father then appeared on Gideon, riding from behind and then galloped around to the front and ahead of the carriage.

"What was this?" questioned Ella with great curiosity. She wondered at Father's energy and demeanor.

"The wagons will arrive tomorrow, but right now, I have a surprise for you, Eleanor," he called to her a bit short of breath as he reached the front steps.

Father dismounted, saying "In fact, I have more than one surprise for you, but first, here is your gift." He gave her a large box tied loosely with a bright blue satin ribbon.

"Oh, this ribbon is gorgeous, Father," she exclaimed. "I cannot wait to tie up my hair with it!"

"Hurry, hurry," he urged, looking back, over his shoulder.

She wondered at the urgency, wanting to savor this singular event with her Father whom she had missed so dearly. Nevertheless, she quickly opened the box, revealing a filmy light blue dress inside, made of sendel, the rarest, and thinnest silk, trimmed in re-embroidered lace at the hem and sleeve points.[27]

Father looked satisfied at her reaction: "Now go up and change into the dress. I have someone for you to meet." He hesitated. Ella waited, a questioning look on her face.

"Ah, well, I have something to tell you. I brought home a new mother for you. In fact, she is arriving now in that carriage."

Eleanor tried to school her face in order to hide her dismay. A new mother? How could this be? Just a moment before, she had been happy!

Changes

Almost numb, she turned to go upstairs to her rooms to change into her new dress in order to present herself to this new woman her father designated 'mother'.

She climbed the stairs to her chambers and went through the motions of dressing. She emerged from her rooms in her new dress, looking and feeling beautiful despite her anxiety. She could hear voices downstairs, and it sounded like more than just her father and one woman. She stopped to listen. It sounded like someone was complaining. The voice belonged to a young woman.

"I am tired, and I cannot believe we have to stand here and wait for someone who did not have the decency to greet us properly," came from a young woman's voice.

"Did he tell us we were coming to the country, Mama?" complained a different young woman's voice, quite similar to the first. The latter was spoken with emphasis on each syllable. Who were these women? Why were they here?

An older woman's voice answered harshly: "Hush now, both of you. I will not have this ruined because you cannot stand a little discomfort. I am sure his daughter will be easy enough to handle, so let us get this over with."

Ella gulped. Apparently she had more than just a new mother. She took a deep breath and walked forward to the top of the landing. She paused for a moment, then schooled her features and descended the stairs.

"Welcome to our home," she said. "My name is Ella."

Ella looked at the two young women before her, both very pretty despite their lack of warmth or friendliness.

"Ella!" quipped the older daughter. "We once had a servant named Ella. She was a cow." The other daughter failed at stifling a giggle.

Father stepped forward and cleared his throat: "You should use your proper name, Eleanor. Galiena, this is my daughter Eleanor. Eleanor, please meet your new sister, Galiena," he said, gesturing to the taller of the two.

"And this is Isana. Isana, Eleanor," he finished, waving his hand to the younger of the two sisters. "I am sure you will have much in common."

With that he turned and left the room, muttering something about business. Ella looked after him in panic, but his back was already turned.

The footmen carried baggage inside and upstairs to the landing where they waited for further instructions, glancing at Ella, wondering what to do. The new stepmother turned to Ella, and slowly looked her up and down:

"Where are our rooms, Eleanor?" she demanded.

Ella quickly ran through the list of rooms in her mind. None had fresh linens, nor were the fireplaces ready, the windows greased . . . a hundred little things that went into making apartments ready for visitors—much less permanent residents! Her mind raced as her new stepmother began tapping her toe.

"I am not quite sure since we had no warning of your arrival," she began.

"Fine. We will take your rooms," said Galiena, pushing past Eleanor and almost knocking her over. "Tell us where they are."

"And I will have your mother's rooms, as I am now the Lady of the House. "[28]

Please fetch the Housekeeper and send her to me." She, too, marched up the stairs gesturing to the footmen with a haughty lift of her chin.

Ella blanched, but rushed to do their bidding. "I would much rather keep the peace, and sleep in makeshift quarters with Mildred's help for now," she thought. "I can fix things later."[29]

As she turned to go and find Mildred, the Stepmother stopped halfway up the stairs and called out in a commanding voice:

"Tell Cook to send trays up to our rooms." A disapproving look came over Stepmother's features: "I expected food when we arrived and we are quite hungry," she snapped.

Again, Ella considered explaining that she had received no advance notice of their arrival, and thought to mention the time of day -- or rather night -- but changed her mind. For now, she would take care of the immediate needs and try to make sense of the situation. After all, she could help the servants as needed until the necessary help could be gathered and reassigned.[30]

Ella first knocked on Mildred's door, to relate the news. The Housekeeper took one look at Eleanor's face, and immediately donned her long apron and grabbed her ring of keys.

"What is it child?[31] What has happened?" As Ella told her of the arrival in the night of Father ahead of the men and wagons, Mildred started shaking her head.

"Oh Millie, we have no time to talk now, for I have a new Stepmother, and she has two daughters. You are summoned to her chambers," explained Ella.

Before Mildred could say anything, Ella rushed out saying, "I will go fetch Cook, so she can start immediately. Hurry now, and we will talk later." [32]

"Oh dear," she heard from Mildred's mouth as she rushed down the hall on the way to Cook's cottage.

She next repeated the news to Cook, who took more effort to rouse and a longer explanation. Soon enough, Ella dashed back to the kitchen to light the fire in preparation for Cook's needs. Then she scurried to rouse the maids to be ready for Mildred's orders, and to be ready to fill in as needed.

She did not want the household to appear lacking in any respect, nor for Father to feel ashamed of her management.[33]

New Realities

Eleanor thought matters would quickly settle into place, for the household normally ran at a high level of efficiency. She quickly had to admit to disappointment, however, for the new residents kept no schedule. They demanded breakfast made to order and then sent up on trays no matter what time of day they awoke, and each of them wanted individual, personal maids immediately. Ella sent to the village for extra help, but this took time.[34] Meanwhile, she helped where she could in whatever way was necessary.

It never occurred to her to win back her rooms, as she hardly had time to be in her chambers anyway. Scullery maids became housemaids, and housemaids became upstairs or ladies maids, and Ella continued to send Cook's grandson little Jimmy down the road to the village to fetch extra help. The notion of Alwyn becoming her maid was put on hold indefinitely, and it seemed as if everything was topsy turvy.

Meanwhile, as each day became increasingly more hectic, Ella spent time with Cook and Mildred to fill in as needed.[35] "Cut the carrots just like ye do wit' yer roses dearie," Cook told her. "Carrots're thicker, mind ye, but the pressure is much th'same."

Ella soon discovered that everyday kitchen labor was hot and sweaty work. After brushing her hair from off her face a dozen times, Ella tied it up in a towel. She grabbed another towel to use as an apron to wipe her hands, and laughed at the thought of what she looked like half in her own dress, and half in Cook's garb. She had no time for spare thoughts, however, so she set to the task of preparing the food as directed by Cook.

She recalled the days, not too far past when she had to be chased out of the kitchen with a curt word and the snap of a towel. In those memories, she dwelled in the kitchen to experience the warm smell of fresh baked bread, hoping she would be rewarded with a sweet treat or a warm hug. Now she stayed in the kitchen out of necessity, hoping to get the household on an equable footing.[36]

In the meantime, it came time to make the monthly rounds of her father's properties and to attend to the needs of the tenants. She went upstairs to her rooms to take a bath and gather her clothes, only to be greeted by Isana's shrieks.

"What are you doing? Get out!"

"I've come for my clothes. I must change, and. . . " Ella began.

"These are not your chambers. Get out!" interrupted Isana, still in the same shrieking tone. Before Ella had time to react, Isana slammed the door.

What should she do? Ella knocked again, firmly.

"Isa, I really must come in and retrieve my clothes," she called out.

Ella opened the door and looked with dismay at the complete chaos of her rooms.

Dresses and petticoats lay everywhere. Necklaces given to her by her mother hung off tabletops in disarray and shoes were piled on top of one another with no thought to order.37

"What has happened here?" she gasped in dismay.

"Well, you obviously have no use for any of this, so Mama gave it all to us," stated Galiena, who had walked up from behind.

"I am sorry, but…" began Ella.[38]

"You are right, you are sorry!" laughed Galiena in derision. Why don't you go back to the kitchen where you belong?" She sniffed. "You smell bad. Get out!"

"And do not call me Isa, only my friends get to call me Isa," quarreled the younger sister.

Looking at Galiena more closely, Ella noticed that she was wearing the filmy blue silk dress Father had brought back from his Journey. As Ella stood in shock, Stepmother[39] came striding down the Hall. She first looked at her daughters, and then looked pointedly at Eleanor.

"You see dear, I told Galiena and Isana to go through your closet and take what they needed as you obviously do not wear any of your nicer dresses."

"You are much better suited to the kitchen and servant's clothes. Why, look at your hands! You must not have a ladylike bone in your body!" She stopped and looked at Ella closely. "Look at the ashes in your hair and the soot on your face!

Do you enjoy the cinders that are part of your entire appearance? You, with an old makeshift apron on. You were right to give us a common name when you introduced yourself; you just left off the first part, Cinder-Ella!"

The Stepsisters laughed in delight:

"Cinder-Ella . . .CinderElla . . .Cinderella !" they repeated in high-pitched squeals. "Cinderella, what a perfect name!"

Stepmother interrupted: "These clothes are wasted on you, and you cannot possibly expect them to wait to have dresses made for them! I cannot imagine there are tailors of quality in this provincial outpost." She looked at a space of nothingness in front of her nose to show complete disdain.

"My daughters and their beauty are obviously much better suited for what your father can provide." She continued with a sniff. "Now go. I'm sure you can find something much more suitable to wear in the trunks of castoffs in the attic," she added, and turned her back on Ella.

Weary from a long day's series of tasks, Ella backed out of her former rooms, and climbed the stairs to the attic, thinking only of bathing and dressing for the next task on her list. She felt grateful she had packed her mother's clothes and carefully placed them between sheets of thin parchment in stacked trunks. She selected a chemise of soft, bleached flax, and a violet colored tunic the shade of her mother's eyes.

Service[40]

She braided her hair and twisted it on top of her head, thinking briefly of happier days, then hurried downstairs to bathe and dress for her rounds. As she paused at the side door with her basket full of bread and soup, Stepmother appeared.

"What is that you have there?" Stepmother demanded.

"I have the usual bread I take to our tenants for our monthly visit," she answered.[41]

"Did you not think to clear this with me before you so blithely left this house without any notice of your dealings?"

"We have always given food to the families under our care, for it is tradition to watch over those who look to us as stewards and patrons," began Eleanor, but Stepmother interrupted her.

"This is no longer your affair. I am the mistress here, and I will make the decisions. Those lazy peasants do not know what a good life they have.[42] They do not need free food from you. Now put that basket down, and make yourself useful somewhere else."

Ella reacted slowly, not quite believing what she had just heard. She turned towards the other woman, setting the basket on one of the kitchen tables, and then noticed her stepmother staring at her hair.

"Who did your hair?" she asked, glaring at Ella. "Did you have your hair arranged in such a way to show up my daughters?"[43]

"I thought no such thing--" Ella began, reaching her hand up to her braid, but Stepmother was not listening.

"Go upstairs immediately and show Galiena and Isana how to style their hair. I want them to have the best, and I will NOT have a country mouse like you showing them up, do you hear me?"

Ella turned and climbed the stairs. Isana occupied her former rooms, and Mildred had the rooms opposite prepared for Galiena. Ella found the Stepsisters in the drawing room situated between the two girls' chambers. Galiena and Isana sat looking in the large bronze mirror, brushing their hair and giggling together. When she opened the door they ignored her until she told them why she was there. Upon hearing her explanation, they turned as one and started talking simultaneously about who would go first and what they wanted as if she were a ladies maid.

She tried to show them how to arrange their own hair, but ultimately she did it for them.[44] She told them about her experience of looking at the portraits and then practicing the hairstyles with Allie's help, but they did not listen. Instead, they simply demanded she plait and twist their hair like hers and the other women in the region. The same thing happened the next day and the next. It became routine for them to call her like a servant, and then demand she fix their hair.

"Come Cinderella, do my hair this instant," each would say.

Ella had asked Mildred to have new rooms made up for her out of sight of her new family members and to have her mother's trunks moved from the attic into her new chambers. She thought she could simply stay out of sight, but she noticed that lacking the ability to torment her, the Stepsisters plagued the servants with constant complaints and unnecessary tasks.

Running after Galiena's and Isana's demands meant that other household chores remained incomplete, so Stepmother then punished the servants by docking their wages or even having them whipped because the chores were not finished. It seemed the three women practiced cruelty simply for pleasure.

Ella helped in every way that she could, as the ever-changing demands from Stepmother and the Stepsisters continued to be delivered. She stood in for Cook in the kitchen when the hours grew too late, for Cook was too old to stand on her feet for so many hours. Ella tied up her long hair in a cloth, then, lacking a maid's sturdy uniform, she wrapped a second cloth around her hips to protect her clothes. She bade Cook sit in a chair by the fire, who then directed Ella while Ella

stirred the pots in order to give Cook's back a rest. At other times, Ella took the servant's mending in her lap, as there was not much difference between this task and her own sewing projects in the basket by her window seat upstairs. Somehow she had to keep the household together! CatStitch, ever watchful, stayed by her side.

Joy & Sorrow

Each day, Ella looked forward to eventide when she walked through the garden and around the back to her mother's grave. There she sat and wept. Out of sight and hearing of anyone else, she cried so much that her tears ran together and formed a little pool next to the grave. She told her mother her worries and her woes, thinking she might find a solution. Mostly she sat and wept, and the pool grew. Meadowlarks and doves floated down to the pool, drank from it and sang to her a soothing song of solace. [45]

All too soon it came time for her father to travel to the fairs, and he came to the ladies drawing room to ask what he should bring back as gifts.[46] First, he asked Galiena.

"Fine clothes!" she squealed.

He asked Isana who blurted out, "Precious jewels for me!"

"And what will you have, Eleanor?" he asked, looking down at the hearth where Ella sat with CatStitch curled up next to her.[47]

Ella thought for a moment, and said: "I would like the first twig that strikes against your hat on the way home, please Father," she answered softly. CatStitch looked at her mistress, then looked at Father and blinked slowly.

As a successful merchant, trading for precious jewels and fine clothes came as second nature to Father. Baldachin, or brocades with metallic threads, sendel, and the newest satin weaves of the highest quality, and jewels that glistened and retained their luster through the ages were part of his trading venue. Each season, he conducted his business with ease and grew increasingly more prosperous.[48]

The men at arms he took with him made sure the route was safe, as he had doubled the number of wagons he utilized since the previous year. All in all, it was a very successful year, and he returned home, whistling. As he neared the village, he remembered that he had not fulfilled Eleanor's request. With that thought and all at once, a hazel twig from a low hanging tree bent down and struck his hat.[49] He smiled, and called for his men to halt. He stopped, reached up, broke off the same twig, and placed it in his hat.

As usual, CatStitch informed Ella when Father neared the estate, winding her sinuous feline body between her mistress's legs and rubbing the sides of her face against Eleanor's shins. Ella rushed into the house and upstairs to freshen up, but was startled to discover the blue dress Father had given her last year waiting in her rooms. She decided not to question its presence, but gladly donned the gown, feeling like her old self. She came out to the Great Hall to see Stepmother and the Stepsisters also dressed and waiting.

"Ahhh, good," said Stepmother with a smile that bared all her teeth. "You finally decided to dress nicely. I sincerely do not want your Father to think you have been mistreated while he has been gone, simply because you prefer to spend your time in the kitchen and dress like a servant!"[50]

"We didn't like that dress anyway," sniffed Galiena.

"It makes our skin look pasty," chimed in Isana.

"Hush!" commanded Stepmother.

Ella moved to go outside on the steps to await the arrival of Father as per usual, but Stepmother forbade her: "We will not stand outside like commoners, Cinderella. Stay here and mind your manners."

Ella kept quiet as she heard the familiar sound of the men and wagons move up the drive, and then the unmistakable sound of Gideon's hooves stomping up to the door. Father burst in, throwing the doors aside. "Where is my family?" he demanded. He stood in the doorway, holding two boxes in his arms looking about.

He spotted the women, and announced, "Well, well, I have two boxes here. I wonder whose names are on these boxes.[51] Hmmm . . ."

"Oh do not tease us, it is unfair!" squealed Galiena. "I hope you brought me my fine clothes," she whined.

"And my precious jewels," squeaked Isana.

They both pouted, and Father gave in. "Very well, then. This box is for you, Galiena."

He placed the large box in the older daughter's arms. She quickly tore open the box and ran up the stairs with fabric spilling over her arms.

"This box is for you," he said to Isana as he handed her a square box, whereupon she tore it open and began piling up her jewelry, a calculating look on her face.

Meanwhile, Ella stood, looking at her father, her gaze intent:

"Well, Eleanor, what would you have of me?" asked Father, smiling.

He reached up to his hat, pulled out the hazel twig, and handed it to her. Ella smiled with delight at the sight of the hazel tree leaves and the twig that held them.

"Oh thank you, Father," she said as she spontaneously hugged him as tightly as she could reach her slender arms around his broad chest. She felt him sigh and relax as he hugged her. Then she felt him stiffen as he looked up and caught his wife's eye. He loosened his grip, and stepped back.

"Well, it is good to be home indeed. I had a long journey. Let us celebrate! How about the usual honeyed fruit, meat pies, and perhaps some spiced wine to drink? I am sure you have it waiting for the end of the long road!" He rubbed his hands together.

Ella started to reply that she had the traditional family repast waiting with the servants, when Stepmother glided over to Father.

"Nonsense dear. After such an excursion, I am sure you want to come upstairs and rest with me. We will have Cook send up trays for the two of us. You can tell me all about the trade and new wealth you have made."

Stepmother swooped up the stairs without a backward glance, and Father followed.

Tears formed unbidden in Ella's eyes, and she rushed, unnoticed outside through the rose garden and directly to her mother's grave. She knelt on the soft dirt mound, and reached her fingers down into the soil underneath. She inserted the hazel twig at the head of the grave mound. She felt closer than ever to her mother, and as she wept anew, she laid down on the gravesite with one arm outstretched and wrapped around the newly planted hazel tree twig.

CatStitch padded over, and curled up within the circle of her mistress's arm, vibrating with a loud, comforting purr. Copious tears fell from Ella's eyes like summer rain upon the hazel twig, and she felt a bond form between herself and this special little plant.

The hazel twig belonged exactly where it now grew into a tiny sapling, and this instantly became Ella's favorite place and refuge.[52]

Thereafter, during her visits, she spoke freely to her Dear Mother. Emotions welled up within her such that she wept for all the injustices of the previous year. She knew no restraint. She was comforted; as if her Dear Mother held her in her bosom. Her tears continued to fill the little pool, which fed the little sapling, and the hazel sapling grew. In the beginning she brought her gardener's pitcher to feed the little tree, but she soon realized that she had no need for any other water, as the magic pool was enough. It replenished her to unburden herself through weeping, and fed the little tree, too.[53]

Drawing upon the little pool next to the grave, within days, the tender sapling grew into a supple little tree. Once it possessed a straight little trunk with offshoots of branches, a sweet white dove made its nest in the newly sprouted leaves, and sang a little song of woe. It matched the folk songs of the region, which not only offered a particular dance rhythm, but also celebrated the co-existence of joy and sorrow. The dove cooed while she talked, and came to her shoulder when she cried. Curiously, CatStitch never moved to pounce on the bird, and the little white dove showed no fear of the feline at Ella's side. The little tree continued to grow, and as soon as the branches could hold the bird its song became something more.

The little bird asked Ella what she wished for. She thought for a moment. "Oh my. I suppose I would like the others in the household to feel the joy of your song as I do," she exclaimed. "Perhaps it will make their burdens lighter in the same way you have helped me."

Nurse

A sense of peace followed Ella as she turned towards the house, then changed her mind and instead, ducked under a rose arbor at the side of the garden, to emerge on a hedge-lined path leading to Nurse's cottage. She found the old woman sitting in a large rocking chair just outside the open front door with a basket of yarn at her feet.

"Hello child. I've been waiting fer ye. Grab the basket and come inside dear. I'll pour some tea."

Ella dutifully picked up the basket, and sat on a little three-legged stool. She placed her hands in the basket and began to sort through the recently dyed wool, loving the contrasting rough and soft feel of the various skeins. She chose a bundle of soft sage green, and wound the end around her left hand. Nurse came over with two cups of steaming linden flower tea,[54] and sat in her familiar easy chair.[55]

"Ah, the sage. That's a loverly color indeed," she said, nodding. Ella held up her arms, and Nurse began winding the wool between the girl's hands. "Ah, just like life. . . not too tight and not too slack," she said with satisfaction.

As Nurse and Ella quickly moved into a rhythm, Ella began to wonder aloud about her life in general. The older woman listened and gently reacted to Ella's words. While they spoke, the doves from the hazel tree came to the lower sash of the window and began cooing. Meadowlarks joined them and added their voices to the melody. A song began to form, and Nurse hummed along. Ella smiled as yet more birds joined those at the window. Swallows swooped in, forming circles outside and interjecting their part, while sparrows chirruped in counterpoint.[56]

The two women laughed as the birds tweeted a symphony, then flew away in a tremendous flock towards the great house right at the moment when Nurse finished winding off the yarn from Ella's hands into a tidy ball and pinned it.

"I really better get back before some new tragedy occurs without my presence," said Ella laughing half-heartedly.

She flung her arms around Nurse and kissed the woman on both cheeks. Nurse held the girl's face between her hands and rubbed noses like she did when Ella was just a tiny little girl.

Gifts

Comforted, Ella walked back along the path, under the arch in the hedge, and then through the gardens in through the scullery doorway to find the kitchen staff standing enthralled by the bird song emanating from every window, chimney flue, doorway, and rafter.[57] Larks, sparrows, swallows, doves, and house wrens serenaded the servants and workers, who in turn, looked happy and carefree. Cook touched the corner of her apron to her eyes as she listened to the trills, and two of the downstairs maids smiled and sighed as they folded linens. Ella moved through the buttery and into the Great Hall, only to find the same situation in the other rooms, with birds filling the nooks and crannies of open windows and vents in each of those rooms, and again, servants giving pause in their work to listen to the sweet sounds.

What a delight to witness the joy on people's faces. In many instances, Ella could see mouths moving along with unknown words of the melody emanating from throughout the halls in every direction.

Suddenly, a loud shriek could be heard: "What is all this racket!" shouted Stepmother, stepping out from her chambers with annoyance written in every line of her body. She craned her neck upwards, but the songbirds moved just out of sight—singing all the while.

Stepmother dashed into the hall and peered into the drawing room, but once again, the birds ducked into shadow, yet never missing a note. Stepmother moved from room to room in a strange jerking motion, attempting to discover the source of the melodious sounds whose beauty escaped her, but she could not find the source. She demanded the servants tell her where she could find the birds, but was greeted with blank stares or questioning looks.[58]

Meanwhile, the singing continued, and the work of the day became an easy burden.[59] Stepmother finally gave up and announced she would retire to her rooms for the night. As her doors closed, a procession of songbirds flew in through the windows in formation through the Great Hall and into the ballroom whereupon everyone put down their work and went into the ballroom and danced.

Ella laughed with delight, and joined in the merriment. "Thank you, oh thank you indeed," she called as the flock finished their song, and flew out the windows into the failing light of evening. The servants departed with an easy gait, smiling and holding hands, or clapping each other on the back.

After so much tension, the household seemed to settle into its old rhythm after that. Thomas and the stable boys mended fences and tended to the flocks whilst tending to the horses that were stabled or out at pasture.

Cook attempted to train a batch of new scullery maids, but kept having trouble finding time thanks to the continuous stream of ever-changing orders from upstairs.

Mildred tried to keep up with the chaotic pace of the household by ensuring the floors and windows were clean, the fireplaces stocked, and sending messages and orders as quickly as possible.

In the meantime she gracefully dealt with Stepmother's demands, along with standing in as ladies maid at a moment's notice, thus continually requesting additional assistance from other parts of the house to stay on track.

Ella found herself filling in as needed in all areas of homemaking tasks, trying to hold the household together so no one would notice the stress placed on the schedule or the workers. Far too many of her nights found her falling asleep by the fire, working her way through a basket of mending or catching a nap in the kitchen while she kept her eye on a pot of simmering stew for Cook who was simply to tired to remain awake.

Meanwhile, Ella continued to visit the gardens daily, and the grave of her Dear Mother where she found peace and comfort by talking to Mother at the mound of the hazel tree.

She thanked the doves for the glorious songs given to the household, with heartfelt gratitude. The bees slowly hummed in the warm air, lazily moving from red flower to orange blossom to yellow bloom and back to red once again. Their paths could be traced from flower to flower as if laying out a magical, sweet trail. They slowly made their way around Ella as if waltzing through the air. She smiled at their dance as she made her way to the tree.

One day the dove in the hazel tree cocked its head to the side as it sang, and offered again to grant any wish. Thinking of her Dear Mother, tears welled up in Ella's eyes. The dove hovered in the air, and gently rested on her shoulder. It nestled against her ear and offered to grant her any wish.

"I do not need anything," she thought as she pondered the sweet bird's generous offer. "Dear bird, you are too kind, but I cannot think of any need." "If I were to ask of anything from you it would be for the golden locket my Dear Mother wore around her neck. I cannot imagine the Stepsisters have noticed it or would notice its absence."

"Ella! Deary, I am needin' yer help!" she heard Cook call from the scullery door. When she looked back at the hazel tree, the sweet dove had disappeared, so Ella hurried to the kitchens to help Cook.

Afterwards, the day wore on in the usual manner: she met with Millie, fixed Galiena and Isana's hair after unsuccessfully attempting to teach them how to do it for themselves, and then she and Allie hung from the rafters in her chambers dried hyacinth out of the garden. After she had dismissed Allie for the evening, Ella returned to the garden to visit her Dear Mother's grave once more.

Upon arriving at the gravesite, she noticed the little bird held a small golden locket hanging from a slender chain. The dove bowed its head, and as Ella knelt in front of the tree, the dove quietly dropped the locket into her lap and flew to its normal, higher perch, cooing softly. Ella reverently placed it around her neck as tears of joy began to flow.

"Thank you," she murmured gratefully to the dove and the hazel tree both, as she curled up around the grave mound, feeling closer to her Dear Mother than ever before. CatStitch came and cuddled up with her purring in tune with the beating of Ella's heart.

On the very next day, again the bird offered to grant any wish, and Ella held onto the locket and smiled in response. "Dear sweet bird. Why do you give me such blessings?"

The dove responded with a song, "It's all about remembering joy and love, and a desire to understand the joy and love.

"Could you perhaps sing something to remind me of my Dear Mother?" asked Ella.

The sweet little dove blinked slowly, and then began an utterly beautiful melody that recalled Ella to her past. The tune carried her to a time when her Dear Mother held her in her arms, kissed her goodnight, hugged her close, and rocked her to sleep. A thousand memories flitted across her mind, and she thought she could smell her mother's rose perfume. She began humming along with the bird when another joined it on the limb just above them; harmonizing with the first dove. After a gentle pause, a pair of gray doves fluttered down from the nearby trees and joined in, adding their voices. The little group of birds continued to sing as more birds began arriving, harmonizing, adding dissonance and depth to the song. Calandra larks and greater and lesser short-toed larks joined in, several crested larks perched high on the tree began singing a much higher and yet still more beautiful sound. Meadowlarks, skylarks, and swallows landed around Ella and near the little pool of water by the grave and joined in, creating a hauntingly beautiful sound as their voices merged with the others; the doves with their cooing and the larks with their melodious whistles and tones. Finally, the woodlarks joined in, perching themselves on her shoulders, softly singing, a tremendous lullaby. The sound was both calming and energizing. As it ended, and silence once again filled the air. She could feel the beauty still lingering throughout the garden.[60]

"Thank you," she whispered, and the flock flew quietly away.

An Invitation

Ella's life once again settled into a recognizable pattern, and the days passed by. One morning Ella woke up early to walk about the garden while the first morning dew still clung to the grass along the borders with CatStitch joyfully padding along behind, happy to help select stems for the household floral arrangements. She moved among the rose bushes with her special clippers in her hand, selecting the blooms for the vases in the hall, and noticed the overly large flowers, heavy fruit, and the bees; she realized spring had arrived. She had not noticed the changing season. In the same moment, she heard a carriage come up the drive along with more than the usual commotion. Her own good feelings caused her to delay going in to see what the ruckus was about.

When she came in by the side door as usual, placing the clippings on the large table in the preparation room next to the kitchen, she could hear excited voices in the hall.

"What is it?" she asked.

"Sometin' to do wit t'festival, Miss," answered Tillie, one of the scullery maids.

Ella hung her gardening apron on a hook, tucked her hair back, and hurried into the hall to join the conversation. She saw Arthur just letting out a messenger dressed in the King's livery. As the door closed, Stepmother held a letter in her hand. The woman actually smiled as she raised the parchment high and read aloud:

Before Stepmother finished reading the missive, Galiena and Isana could be heard throughout the house shrieking and talking over her words.

"I can't believe this! I'm so excited!" said Galiena, snatching the letter out of her mother's hands.

"Me too!" echoed Isana as she tried to peer over Galiena's shoulder.

"But what will I wear, how shall I dress?" Galiena looked to her mother.

"I think I will tell father to get me new fabric!" rushed Isana, now tugging on the letter.

"I would hate to disappoint my future husband," crowed Galiena, looking back at the letter as she held it out of Isana's reach.

"You may dance with him first, but I will win his heart" called Isana, now noticing Ella. "Good thing we have you to do our hair…I mean MY hair, since you will just be the sister of the Princess," now looking at Galiena with a wicked grin.

"Oooh, I will show you," hissed Galiena. "You'll see when the Prince can't stop gazing at me in wonder and doesn't even notice you, you, you. . . cow! You are a cow—a double cow, yeah, and cows don't need hair!" she shrieked.

"Hush! We must start preparing immediately," shouted Stepmother.

"May I see the invitation?" asked Ella.

"You, Cinderella? What would you know about a Royal Invitation?" demanded Stepmother.

"If you please Stepmother,"" answered Ella, "It is time for the annual festival, and we all attend every year. Even the servants attend. Our royal family joins in the local activities when they have a special event like when Prince Christophe was born, and now this, his search for a bride. We have not attended the last couple years because of, well, because…." Her voice trailed off.

Ella pointed to the invitation. "See, here, where it mentions regalia? I can show you my dress." Her eyes lit up at the thought, until Stepmother snatched the piece of parchment out of her hand.

"How dare you keep this information from me! And as for your pitiful dress, you cannot show it to me because I had it burned when I first saw that ridiculous piece of country nonsense with ribbons and fluff amongst the dresses you gave my daughters."

Ella chose to ignore the statement that she had "given away" her dresses, but the thought of her beautiful, cherished festival dress having been burned brought hot tears to her eyes. [61]

"What absolute nonsense," continued Stepmother. She turned and faced Ella in wrath, "Oh stop those tears at once, Cinderella, do you hear me? Now! I would never let anyone from this house appear in a country costume. Never, do you hear me? Never!"

"But my mother had a traditional dress, like that, too," started Eleanor.

"Not any more. I am your mother. Besides, do you think I kept any of the trunks you left behind in the attic? Absolutely not. I told Thomas to burn everything. Every. Single. Thing. Now get away from my sight.

Gratitude[62]

"I have things to do if one of your sisters is going to be the future queen, and I do not need you to get in the way. I do not even want to see you, do you hear me?" Stepmother screamed, and pushed her face up close, in front of Ella's face. "You disgust me, and I do not want to look at a girl who did not see fit to tell me about something so important as an *Annual Festival*."

"With all respect, you are not listening," tried Ella.

"Leave me!" hissed Stepmother between clenched teeth.[63]

The household descended into uproar as Stepmother began issuing orders to servants all at once, regardless of rank or assigned duties.

Ella stumbled up to her rooms by a little used stairway, and sat in her window seat looking over the gardens. CatStitch joined her, curling up on her lap to provide comfort.

The sweet dove from the hazel tree landed just outside on her window ledge. In its beak hung her Dear Mother's cherished golden locket. Holding the locket in its beak, the sweet dove began to sing the melody of her mother's lullaby.

Lullay lullow, lullay lully,
Beway bewy, lullay lullow,
Lullay lully,
Baw me bairne, sleep softly now.[64]

Ella lovingly grasped her Dear Mother's locket and put it over her head and around her neck.

She looked around her rooms, at the bunches of lavender and hyacinth hanging from the beams on the ceiling, at the blankets on the bed; still the same that she and her mother had lain on together so long ago when they talked and whispered combined stories and dreams when Father was gone on his long trips.

Ella sighed, grateful for being surrounded by good memories. She felt grateful for having known, loved, and been loved by such a Dear Mother; Grateful for the lullaby in this moment; Grateful for the locket to keep the memories alive; Grateful for companions and sweet friends.

Festival Preparations & Mayhem

All at once, Alwyn burst through her chamber door, "I am so sorry Miss, but I am not supposed to be here, so I have to hurry, " she gasped.

Whatever is the matter, Allie?" asked Ella.

"The Mistress has pulled me off yer service completely, and says I hafta prepare Miss Galiena and Miss Isana fer the Festival. . . but I don't want ye t' think I'm neglectin' ye, now!"

"Oh, I understand, Allie. Please set your heart at ease. We both know that I can dress myself!"

"But what will ye wear, Miss?"

"I will think of something. Now go and do not get in trouble!"

In actuality, she had no idea what she would wear, and as soon as Allie left, she cried anew, thinking about the festival years before and of dancing with Father, coming home with Mother, and her feelings of being so happy. She realized that she had no idea what the future held, and most of all, that she likely would never again attend a dance, except in her memories.

Sounds from below brought her out of her reverie, so she went to the doorway to listen. The noise and confusion grew louder, culminating in a loud, metallic crash, followed by yelling. She rushed down the center stairway, through the Great Hall and over to the kitchen. The sight before her seemed unbelievable. Cook stood next to the ovens, red in the face, holding a large frying pan in the air as if she would swing it at any moment. Stepmother stood in front of her with her arm extended, finger pointing, accusing Cook of incompetence.

"You are dismissed from service, you old hag!" hissed Stepmother.

"It's not my fault, Missus," cried Cook, now cradling the frying pan against her bosom.

"Pick up that mess you made, and be gone," retorted Stepmother.

"But, you knock'd everythi-" attempted Cook.

"I did not ask for your opinion!" screeched Stepmother, suddenly noticing Ella walking through the buttery. She snorted and flounced out of the room, leaving the mess on the floor.

Ella looked into the kitchen, noting an incredible mess that must have been the intended dinner for the night, now on the floor, and more: somehow, live chickens were loose in the kitchen! The pots hung all askew from their hooks, and the lentils which had been sorted into two bowls and waiting to be soaked were now upended into and combined in the ashes of the fireplace, and the chickens were tripping over the bowls!

Ella sighed as CatStitch instantly ran between her legs, and started pouncing on the chickens, whose focus had been the lentils in the fireplace . . . until the cat came into their midst. Once CatStitch descended, the chickens panicked, and everything became wings flapping and fur flying, meowing and clucking! Ella didn't know whether to laugh or sigh yet more deeply, but decided first she must console Cook.

Just as she began to place her arms around the older woman, Stepmother came storming back into the kitchen, stabbing her finger in Ella's direction:

"You pick up those lentils!" she shrieked. "And get those chickens out of here. Why did you let them in here in the first place you old fool!?"

"But you—" said Cook

"How dare you talk back to me!?" Stepmother's voice trembled, and she flung her arms out, sweeping the bowls and pans asunder, back to the floor that Ella had just picked up off the floor and stacked back on the counter.

"Why are the rushes so old and look at the lentils all over the flook!" she continued. "You are about as useful as this old woman," she barked at Ella, gesturing at Cook.

"Lentils. Rushes. Pots." Stepmother stated, emphasizing each word with a poke at Ella's chest, looming over the girl, with her face up close. She suddenly stood up and narrowed her eyes: "And get that mangy cat out of here!"

CatStitch paused and looked at Stepmother with one big yellow eye, while neatly swatting at a chicken trying to get into the buttery. Stepmother scowled and stormed off once again. Ella paused for a moment, closed her eyes, and took a deep breath. She thought about what needed to be done. She opened her eyes to find Cook waiting to speak.

"Miss, her Ladyship, accused th'others a stealin' eggs, and I protested I did. It just warn't right, it warn't. And herself marched out t'th'coop, to count th'eggs, and next thing ye knows, t'th'chickens, well, they got loose, and her ladyship starts t'screamin' about th'muck—in th'coop, mind ye! Where else would muck be, I ask ye? Me girls all scattered, and well…I guess ye knows th'rest."

"I know Cook, I know. Now don't fret," soothed Ella. "Let's just get this mess tidied up, and all will be well."

Cook started to bend down, holding on to her back as she did so: "I'll start with these lentils, sose I can get th'soup goin' fer supper."

Ella placed her hands on Cook's shoulders and lifted her up gently. "Now," Ella softly uttered to the old woman. "Call your girls, and then go fetch Thomas to gather fresh rushes please. Then come back and we'll get supper going."

"CatStitch, go find Jimmy and tell him to come here immediately to take these chickens back to the coop."

The cat did not look happy at this turn of events, for having chickens so available in the scullery seemed a marvelous idea, but darted off nevertheless. Meanwhile, Tillie arrived, and Ella directed her to gather the frightened chickens in one place to await Jimmy's arrival. Next she whistled the tune she heard the birds sing in the garden, and was happy to hear an answering whistle along with a corresponding rustle of flapping wings.

Ella looked to the windows at the arriving birds, and asked: "Could you please help me by collecting the lentils and peas that have fallen in the ashes? You can eat the small ones if you would like."

The birds quickly began working in pairs, and Ella set about collecting the pots from off the floor, trying to imagine the scene that had played out before she arrived. CatStitch returned ahead of Jimmy, and appeared delighted to help Tillie with keeping the chickens penned up in one place.

Suddenly, Stepmother returned once again. She flew into the kitchen, shrieking and waving her arms around, whereupon the songbirds retreated into the pantry.

"Why have the rushes not been replaced?" she demanded. "And what are these pots and pans doing all over the place? How can anyone think to run a proper household like this? No wonder you are such a mess!" she railed at Ella and turned, only to step on an errant chicken. She flailed about, knocking most of the pots off the table once again, along with the two bowls of gathered lentils and peas, back onto the floor.

CatStitch yowled loudly as the chickens got loose once again, and Stepmother yelled: "This is inexcusable! I only came back for hot water, and this is what I find!" Glaring at Ella, she spoke between clenched teeth, "Since your servants are useless, bring me the hot water yourself."

Stepmother turned to leave at the same moment that CatStitch darted out of the pantry to block the path of an escaping chicken. Seeing the woman in her path, CatStitch tried to stop, but instead skidded across the floor and under Stepmother's dress, bracing herself against the woman's legs with her claws. Stepmother screamed as she jumped, with CatStitch now climbing up her legs, entangled in her petticoats. The woman landed on a chicken whose squawks mingled with her screams. As she fell, her arm knocked over a row of glass bottles waiting on the shelf of the buttery: filled with warm milk. They tumbled one at a time like dominoes, and shattered on the floor all around her. A few tipped and broke upon the shelf first, dripping milk into Stepmother's hair.

Meanwhile, CatStitch remained trapped underneath Stepmother's dress, and now had decided to exit by way of the tunic sleeve, which was more than uncomfortable for both the frantic, yowling cat and the hysterical, screaming woman. Finally, CatStitch extricated herself from Stepmother, looked around, and saw Ella standing there in consternation. The cat noticed the milk, and began lapping it off the floor, purring.

When the older woman gathered herself up off the floor trying to avoid the broken glass, spilt milk, and the chickens pecking at her feet, she looked up to see Ella standing there, and CatStitch at her feet who paused momentarily to look at her then slowly blink her yellow eyes. All was silent for a moment except for the clucking of chickens, the sound of birds pecking at lentils, and milk dripping off both Stepmother and broken glass bottles. Ella held her breath.

"It is fortunate for you," Stepmother said crisply, "that I have more important things to worry about and that I need your help, or you would face severe consequences for what has just happened. I will deal with this later. Right now, you will get this place under control and be useful."

"I am sorry. I am trying to help," offered Ella, glaring at CatStitch and unsuccessfully shooing her away.

"Well, when you have finished picking up your mess, you need to teach these useless servants to get busy; nothing is ready for tonight!" and Stepmother stomped out the door and up the stairs.

Ella sighed and turned to continue her tasks. The birds came back in full force to help, and as she went to fill a pot with water in order to place it on the fire to warm. Cook returned with Thomas.

Cook patted Ella on the cheek, clucking like the chickens as she did so. Ella left, followed by Thomas carrying the pot of hot water behind her. They delivered the water then turned to go.

"Where are you going?" demanded Galiena.

"Well, I need to prepare for the festival, too."

"Ha! Cinderella, going to the ball! What an outrageous idea! You smell like lentils and peas!"

"She looks like a boiled lentil!" inserted Isana. The stepsisters looked at each other and laughed.

"Now look what you've done," Galiena accused Ella, "You made me laugh, so my makeup will crack, and my hair will fall out of place. You planned it this way."

"It does not matter, the Prince is only going to look at me, anyway," jeered Isana.

"Ha! You are just a foolish girl. It is written in the stars, that I will be queen, and Mother agrees with me, do you not, Mother? Mother!! Where are you, Mother. . . MOTHER!!!"

The two girls left the room screaming for their mother.

Not long after, Ella heard them assemble in the Hall. It sounded like they were ready to leave, and leave without her! She hurried to the gallery above the Great Hall, and peered over the rails. Stepmother looked up at her, taking in her obvious dishevelment:

"Well!" Stepmother said with a small little smile. "I suppose you have been in your true element today Cinderella."[65]

"I was planning on joining you at the festival, Stepmother."

"Oh, that is too bad, Cinderella, you could go if you were ready, but we are leaving and you have no ride. Perhaps tomorrow. Good-bye."

Ella sank to her knees in dismay. "Why did I think I would attend the festival at all?" she thought.

She pulled herself up and looked out the window, out over the gardens, to watch the evening light roll across the landscape, and closed her eyes.

Festival Night One

Ella imagined the festivities in town. As she stood at the window gazing into the night, she heard doves cooing, so she followed the sound to the little grotto formed by her Mother's grave, the hazel tree and the little pool. As she approached, an overwhelming scent of roses greeted her, and she beheld rose petals strewn across the surface of the pool, the water rippling in a gentle breeze. She knelt, and dipped her fingers in the scented water, then placed her rosy wet fingers over her eyes to offer them relief from the day's events. All her cares seemed to slip away. She rose from the side of the pool, and raised her arms with the warmth of the breeze that now moved from the tree and across her neck and shoulders.

A surge of energy coursed through her body, and she smiled at the feeling that now made her heart race. She looked at the hazel tree, which shook in the wind as each leaf rustled individually of its own accord. The moon was just rising, and it cast a silvery glow up until twilight's last minutes. She saw her sweet dove friend coast in with the warm breeze, cooing softly.

The sweet dove landed on the branch of the hazel tree just in front of her and asked what she wished for. This time, she knew exactly what to say.

> *"Little tree, little, please shake over me,*
> *Help me be worthy of any help you can send my way."*

The breeze still blew. The sweet little dove continued to coo. The leaves of the tree shook. Then suddenly, all was still.

And there, lying within the branches of the tree lay a beautiful dress spun of gossamer thread the color of silver moonbeams with diamonds shaped like dew drops sewn across the neckline. More jewels ran across the girdle and the hemline like the stars in the sky. The chemise was made from the softest of sendel silks she had ever witnessed or dreamed of.

Ella hardly dared touch it. She knew it was hers as surely as anything could be known, so she lifted it up and over her head while her kirtle and daytime chemise instantaneously dropped to the ground. The dress enfolded her as if it were a second skin.

As she reveled in the luxurious feel of the whisper soft layers next to her skin, the dove flew over to the hazel tree and back with a pair of silver slippers hanging by glittered ribbons from its beak.

The slippers dropped at her feet, and she slipped them on with ease. She instantly felt a tingling sensation wind around her body and up to her neck, and then to her head. She reached up her hands to find her hair brushed and loose all around her with a diamond circlet to hold it in place. She felt beautiful, and she knew her mother would be proud of the way she looked. How wonderful it felt!

She turned in a full circle, enjoying the feel of the skirt as she spun! While she turned, she looked around the clearing and suddenly her shoulders lowered, for she knew not how she would travel to the village square. Just then, Thomas pulled around in the older carriage, with two matched bays harnessed to the front:

"Climb aboard, milady, your carriage awaits!" called Thomas exaggeratedly, as he leapt down from the seat. Jimmy stood on the sash, dressed in the former family livery:

Thomas bowed low, then let down the step, and handed her to Jimmy, who helped her into the carriage through the door sash. Ella felt as though she were walking into a dream as she touched her hand to Thomas' for balance and stepped into the vehicle. She carefully arranged her delicate skirts as she sat down, and Thomas closed the door, jumped back up to the coachman's step and up to the seat once again. He called out to the horse yoked at the front:

"Hiya! Let's go!" and they were off!

Thomas pulled the carriage to a standstill at the entrance to the city gate. The path from there led directly to the Town Square, where the Village Leaders had erected a pavilion between the columns for the festivities. Ella could hear the sounds of the fiddle and pipe, and it sounded like a harpist had been added, too. The *Maiden's Dance* had just begun.

A wave of melancholy briefly washed over her as she recalled the past, but she forced herself to smile as Thomas lifted her out of the cart, and she turned to walk towards the square.[66] Thomas reminded her of the importance of meeting at the gate before the festival ended for the night, and she nodded as she glided away.

Once she arrived at the square, she remained hidden among the clematis vines that lined the outer pillars of the square, watching her friends and neighbors enjoy themselves in dance and merriment for a few moments. She searched until she found Stepmother, Galiena, and Isana standing at the sidelines looking vaguely disdainful. Just as she was about to step out to join the crowd, someone noticed her, and the whispers started circulating.

"Who is that beautiful girl?"

"Who is that mystery woman over there under the flowers?"

"Who is that lovely woman?"

Somehow, due to her absence from the festival the preceding two years, or because of her magical aura: no one recognized her, so she moved about with ease. The whispers of the presence of a most beautiful young woman soon reached the Prince, and he made his way to her, wondering what he would find. The Prince bowed and Ella curtsied.

Prince Christophe asked, "May I have the pleasure of this dance My Lady?"

Ella laid her hand in the prince's outstretched hand, and he swept her out to the floor where they joined the Contra-formation. Ella turned to the side in single step, as the Prince stepped backward with a bransle-single step.

The two moved forward in double step, joining arms as they wove between the other couples on the floor, and marked the pavane pattern in time to the music. The music slowed, and Christophe swung Ella to face him, and she half-stepped to his side, whereupon they placed their palms together, inner arms raised, and circled their jointly raised arm as if it were a pole.[67]

"From where have you traveled, Sweet Princess?" asked Christophe.

"I am not a Princess, Your Highness, but live within your lands," answered Ella.

"Ah, a mystery woman. I am intrigued. What is your name, then, fair maiden? Who is your family?"

"I have no mother, and my father travels far and wide."

Prince Christophe looked puzzled, and Ella laughed and continued with the dance steps. She and Christophe faced each other and touched both palms then backed-stepped to the left, changed partners, turned, and came together.

They back-stepped to the right, changed partners, turned and came together once again. They joined arms for the finale, ended in the pavane pattern, a single step and the music ended. Prince Christophe bowed and tossed his hair back smiling, and Ella curtsied. Her smile flung new dimensions of brilliance throughout the room, and those in attendance took note.

"Please, I must have the next dance," blurted the Prince, and Ella laughed with delight, not noticing the glares she received from the other women in the room, especially from the Stepsisters.

The next dance was a Morris Dance,[68] which left no room for any talking, but the two could not seem to take their eyes off one another. The rest of the folk at the festival could not seem to take their eyes of Ella and the Prince! The next song was quite as lively, and finally, during the following song, they formed the pattern for a Court Dance and had time to dance much closer and hear each other's voices.

Prince Christophe asked her if she knew about the local dance traditions, and she told him about the *Maiden's Dance* and her own experience.

He watched her eyes light up with joy as she talked about the music, the flowers, and the generations of mother-daughter sharing. She asked if he had any special tradition that struck his memory, and he thought a moment.[69] Then she saw a sparkle come into his eye.

"When I was young, each year on my birthday, my parents would hide my presents all over the castle. It would take the entire day for me to find them. It was such a wonderful game, trying to hunt down my gifts, with my father giving me clues. . . some of them helpful and some of them sending me on wild goose chases.

"It is fun to think of our early childhood is it not. It strikes me that you are no ordinary woman, and were never an ordinary girl!"[70]

Ella nodded, thinking about how nice it was to have this glimpse into his memories and to see the carefree look on his face.

"Right now, it is so easy to answer that I am grateful for the tradition that says the future king must always choose his bride from among the maidens of the kingdom, else I would never have met you.[71] I cannot remember when I have enjoyed myself more than this past hour dancing and laughing with you tonight." Ella looked into his eyes and felt herself blush. It had not occurred to her until now that she had spent all her time with the prince exclusively, yet it felt so natural.

"Please, do not be alarmed. I hope I was not too forward in what I just said. I only meant to say that you have made me very happy tonight just to be able to talk and laugh.

"I feel the same way too, Your Highness."

"Oh, please! Will you call me Christophe? Certainly if we are holding hands, we can go by our first names. Oh, wait, I do not believe you have given me your name! My Beautiful Lady, will you tell me your name?"

"I think I quite like being the Woman of Mystery," laughed Ella.

Just then, the Lord Chamberlain of the King stepped up to the platform, which had been erected under the pavilion, and reminded everyone that the festival would be extended two more nights in honor of Prince Christophe. He announced that the next night's festivities would be held in a special canopy erected in the flower fields on the other side of the village on the road leading to the royal castle. Prince Christophe turned to ask Ella if she would be there the next night, but she was gone.

The clock struck midnight.

As much as she wanted to stay until the end of the festivities, Ella knew she needed to be at home when the others arrived. She walked briskly away from the Town Square to the City Gate to meet Thomas. He helped her into their makeshift carriage, and set off at a quick pace. When she arrived home, Ella rushed upstairs, and changed into a soft white chemise and deep rose-colored tunic. She slipped her feet into her garden shoes, then rushed down the stairs and out to the garden with her amazing silver gown and shoes in her arms.

She stood under the tree, and flung the clothing up, into the branches. Ella watched as the moonbeams, sparkling with stardust, shone down upon the garden and lit up the hazel tree so bright that she could not discern the moment when the dress and slippers disappeared.

One moment she held them in her arms and flung them upwards. In the next moment, they merged with the flashing, sparkling light of the tree. The glow from the moon sparked, and little silver stars shot out from the tree in an arc, landed in the little pool and on the flowers surrounding her Dear Mother's grave. Peaceful darkness followed.

The magical dress and slippers no longer remained, but her memories of the night endured, and Ella sat down next to the mound and hurriedly spoke of the miraculous dress, the spectacular sights, the new dance steps and music so rich and full. Most of all she told her Dear Mother of her time with Prince Christophe that made her heart swell with rapture and sing more loudly than ever her voice could put tunes to words. And oh, Prince Christophe: so charming and courteous, so funny with a smile so genuine, and yes, so handsome! She sighed with delight.

She dared not stay, however, so she tiptoed back to the house, in through a side door and upstairs to her rooms to lie down, and dream of the wonderful night. She heard Stepmother and the Stepsisters enter the house shortly thereafter, but stayed quiet in the dark lest they come looking for her.

Festival Night Two

The next morning she made no comment as Stepmother and the Stepsisters complained about the mystery woman at the festival. She wanted to prepare for the festival as she had not been able to the previous day, but Stepmother declared the day be set aside for drastic measures to be sure to attract the Prince. Ella's help was mandatory.

"Cinderella, I will hold you personally responsible for making your sisters presentable. Their hair was fine, but I noticed that the other young women had ribbons and trim on their dresses, and I blame you for not taking care of that. I want trim on their dresses today."

Ella thought about the previous conversation where she had tried to explain the local tradition of the dance, and wondered how she could explain that the dress was related to the dance. Ella recalled how her Dear Mother and Mrs. Henderson had placed ribbons on her dress, some starting from her shoulders, hanging loosely to her elbows or waist, where others would be placed to hang to her knees. The colors would have to complement the dress, yet allow for the entire ensemble to flow and blend itself into one as the dancer moved. How would she ever successfully convey this message? She brought a basket of ribbons to the drawing room, and tried to referee the subsequent argument that ensued. Ultimately, she left the room when they banished her, as they claimed she distracted them from their beauty routine. As she left the room, Galiena called out,

"And what are you going to do tonight while we entertain the Prince?"

"Why, I plan on joining you tonight," answered Ella.

"You, Cinderella? Whatever will you wear?"

"I will wear the blue dress Father gave me that you do not like."

Ella turned to leave, her heart aching for the bustling servants, who were trying to fulfill every command issued to them.

"Get it right!" yelled Galiena as she squirmed when Allie started brushing her hair.

"Ow! You hurt me!" squealed Isana as Tillie inadvertently yanked on a tangle. Isana yanked the brush out of the maid's hand and threw it across the room.

Time disappeared as Ella spent the day solving problems, averting disasters, and smoothing over misunderstandings. By the time she crept upstairs to prepare for the night's festivities, she realized the others were leaving out the front doors and settling themselves in the family carriage amidst laughter and high-pitched stories of anticipation.

Shoulders drooping, she entered her room, resigned to reliving the wonderful memories from the previous night. This was further confirmed when the first sight that greeted her was the filmy blue dress laid out on the bed, with a large wine stain spread across the entire front of the dress! Ella took a deep breath that was part cleansing breath and part sigh, and changed her mind.

Instead of lying down on her bed in resignation, she would go to her Dear Mother's grave for comfort. She tripped down the stairs, out through the garden and came to the beautiful grotto to find the tree once again shaking in the breeze.

Dear little Hazel Tree, shaking with life,
Please tell me, in my sorrow,
What should I do?

Ella heard the cooing of her Sweet Dove friend, and suddenly and once again, lying within the branches of the tree, a dress appeared for her to use. This one was woven from metallic gold threads shot through the beautiful ivory fabric. Crystals and beads adorned the trim. Silk petticoats underneath matched the sleeves and made a swishing sound as the dress moved.

The early evening moon played games of light on the leaves above her head as the fabric surrounding the images soaked in the excess light, creating a sense of incredible depth and beauty as it moved towards her.

The dress last night was so beautiful she felt like she walked on air as she wore it, Now, this dress was soft and filmy to the touch in a much different way. As she played with it between her fingertips she became aware of the fabric reaching towards her body and melding itself to her as she moved. This was a dress made for dancing! She lifted it over her head as before, and it melted over her like a fluid memory that sways with any movement and embraces the dance steps within its folds.

The sweet dove flew over to her with a pair of embroidered bronze silk slippers in its beak. Once again, as she placed her feet inside the slippers, her hair swirled around her head in an intricate mass of braids and artfully arranged cascading curls. What a delight!

"Thank you, so much!" she called out in glee.

Ella spun around and the dress crackled and flashed in the air like sparks of golden and white lightning mixed with sunshine even though the sun had set. She laughed in delight, and then hurried down to the front drive to meet Thomas and Jimmy waiting for her with the old carriage once more. The distance was further, but Thomas knew the back roads, and they arrived shortly after the beginning of the festivities.

Ella looked up at the peaks of tents positioned in front of her; some of which towered well over five times her height and were as tall as the family chateau.

The bustling sounds of people talking, flirting, and prancing around had her giggling in delight as she smelled roasting pheasant and pork on nearby fires. She carefully navigated her way through the ropes holding the pavilions poles upright and into the throng of people. Hundreds of people milled around, and many of them had traveled more than a fortnight to be present at the festival. The musicians, bards, and jesters paced through the crowd, pleasing and dancing merrily with anyone who would share a little amount of coin.

Ella entered through the main arch, and calmly walked through the crowd despite the whispers of awe and the speculation about who she was because as she entered, Prince Christophe immediately left his chair and began walking towards her. He had eyes for no one but her. The smile on her face seemed to have been made for him alone.

He walked purposefully towards her and bowed.

Eleanor curtsied.

Prince Christophe looked deep into her eyes and said, "I am so glad you kept your promise and returned to me.

"I never break my promises," she replied, smiling.

He offered his hand and took her out onto the dance floor where the Basse Dance was just beginning. She radiated joy as she made her way to his side and began the dancing/walking movements.

The two danced for several songs, alternating between the lively, fast paced and energized songs: the Sellinger's Round, the Official Branie among them, to slow and stately, fine tuned songs, like the Black Alman. Their hands did not always touch, but their flirting back and forth and close proximities made the air between them feel like it was electrified and super charged. They never switched partners beyond the dance parameters, and stayed within a short arm's reach away, spinning around the area as if there were no one else there.

"I wonder what he likes," thought Ella as a song started that required them to remain somewhat close to each other.

"Tell me about yourself" she whispered as he got closer.

"What would you like to know?" he replied, smiling

They spoke about the costumes surrounding them, which turned to colors and fabric for a short while, each commenting on the other's garb; but soon turned into hobbies, and interests. Ella made sure to conceal her true identity whilst still remaining true and honest to the Prince.
When she appeared in the main feast area the discussion amongst the crowd quickly became centered on discovering her identity. The tables were laid out with a magnificent assortment of foods ranging from the roasted boar, glistening with fat and spices in the firelight, to succulent fruits from the countryside, cut and laid out onto silver platters that had been dressed for the king. The silver of the platters and plates twinkled in the night as the candlelight and fires played on their polished surfaces.

Everyone talked about the beautiful, mysterious woman from the night before, and then were startled to see her once again walking with the Prince that very night.

As the evening started to close, Ella knew it was time to go. The Lord Chamberlain announced the final night of the ball would be the next night, at the castle. Before the prince could stop her, she darted out of the entrance and disappeared in the darkness.

The clock struck midnight.

Upon arriving home with Thomas' help once again, Ella quickly raced through the house and upstairs to change her clothes, then outside to the rose garden and around the back to the grotto. The dress slowly started to drift up and off of her as she ran closer to the tree; she also slipped off her bronzed shoes and turned to see them slowly melt into the earth and disappear without a sound.

She quickly put on her old brown kirtle and slipped her feet into her regular wooden shoes. She saw the dress once again on the mound where her Dear Mother was buried.

> *Thank you, Dear Mother.*
> *Thank you Little Hazel Tree.*
> *Thank you Sweet Dove.*
> *My life is so blessed because of you.*

Whispering a final thank you, she skipped back inside through the side door in her chemise and kirtle, and ran upstairs to dream once again of such a perfect night.

Festival Night Three[72]

Eleanor awoke refreshed from the exciting goings on from the night before, followed by gentle dreams. She felt determined that on this, the final day of the festival, she would find a way to prepare for the festivities and join the family in her true identity.

She missed soaking her hands in the special apricot paste that Alwyn made previously, so she set about making it for herself.[73] She gathered the mortar and pestle in the kitchen, the other ingredients from the butlery, then sat back down and began to work the apricots into a paste. The longer she worked it she gave it a more translucent appearance, an amazing fruity smell, and a smooth texture when it hardened. Once she had enough to soak her hands and nails, she stood up to leave-- only to run into Stepmother.

"Here you are. I ought to have known you would be hiding in the kitchen when I needed you to fix Galiena's and Isana's hair before the festival and ball tonight.

"There will be no fancy hair halfway up and halfway down. I want their hair falling down their backs like that dreadful mystery woman," ordered Stepmother. She looked at the porcelain bowl in Ella's hands.

"What is this?" she hissed

"Nothing of any importance. This is just a home remedy or potion that I have used in the past for my hands. I did not think you would like it."

"No, that is polish for your nails!" Stepmother grabbed the bowl from Ella and began walking upstairs. "How dare you try and keep this away from us!" She stomped up the stairs with the bowl of translucent apricot lotion in her hands. Then she halted and turned back, demanding: "This is not complete." Stepmother squinted her eyes; "There is not enough here for us; only for you! Where do you hide your secret concoction?"

Ella calmly replied, "We would need to make more," and she tried to think how she could do so quickly without disturbing the household routine. Ella sighed. "Well," she thought, "I suppose I can ask Little Jimmy to climb up the apricot trees and get some ripe fruit from the orchard."

Ella found Jimmy, asked him to gather a basket of apricots while she prepared the other ingredients for the apricot paste. She went back to the kitchen for the mortar and pestle and began grinding some rosemary, a small amount of pine needles, and other ingredients into a preliminary paste. Just as she finished, she heard a flutter of wings and tweeting from the kitchen door.

She turned around and was surprised to see three meadowlarks fluttering in midair. "Jimmy's in trouble" they chirped, quickly leaving and flying towards the orchards.

Ella began to take off her apron in order to run and check on Jimmy, when Alwyn burst into the room breathlessly:

"Stepmother wants the nail potion immediately, and by the way, why are you making it? Why did you not send for me?"

"I have no time for explanations Allie. Tell her that I have to run to the orchard to get the apricots," and Ella rushed outside.

The meadowlarks were waiting just outside the kitchen garden gate. They fluttered anxiously as she approached, and led her to where Jimmy was lying on the ground next to a broken ladder with his leg twisted at a painful angle. Ella looked up at the birds:

"Thank you sweet birds for your service. Please go fetch Thomas as quickly as possible." The birds immediately flew towards the stables.

Ella knelt next to Jimmy who lay there, silently biting his lower lip.

"All is well. I am here now. We will get you seen to and taken care of Jimmy. Please do not worry." Her words belied her fears, for she had seen injuries like his that became quite serious and crippling, even.

Two goldfinches appeared at that moment with a cloth woven by nurse. Ella reached up to take it from them, but they fluttered in place, tugging the cloth and pulling her towards the back lawns. She realized they wanted her to go to the grotto.

"Just a few moments, Jimmy, I will return shortly."

She lifted her skirts and ran while the goldfinches flew overhead carrying the soft cloth. When she arrived at the little pool, the birds let go of the cloth so that it fluttered down, into the water.

Ella knelt next to the water and washed the cloth in the pool made from holy tears. The leaves of the hazel tree shook and a breeze shimmered over the surface of the water.

Once the cloth was completely saturated, she ran back to Jimmy and tenderly wrapped his crooked leg with the cloth. As she did so and before her very eyes, the bone eased itself back into place, and Jimmy sighed in relief. A sense of peace quickly overtook his features and he closed his eyes.

"So much better," he sighed, smiling weakly.

Meanwhile, Thomas arrived. "Oh, thank goodness, you are here Thomas. Will you take Jimmy to Nurse's cottage so she can tend to him please?

"Of course, lass.

"Do not worry Jimmy," reassured Ella putting her hand on his shoulder "I will stay with you for tonight."

Ella picked up the basket and gathered the scattered apricots, then hurried back to the kitchen where she plopped them into a pot of boiling water for a long minute then quickly drew them out, pulled off the skins and set about making the pulp. She added it to the paste she had already made, and worked it to its proper texture. When she was ready, she trudged upstairs to the Stepsisters.

It was a long day of preparation.

When evening finally arrived, Ella watched Stepmother and the Stepsisters mount the carriage and set off towards the castle. Ella heard a flock of birds approach once again, forming a circular pattern leading her back to the grotto. Her avian friends cooed softly, chirped sweetly, and altogether sang a melodious tune. Ella gazed at her beautiful place of refuge for a moment: sad, but resolute. She needed to go visit Jimmy. She turned and walked towards Nurse's cottage.[74]

Ella knocked on Nurse's cottage door, surprised that she heard laughter emanating from within.

"Come on in Dear," called Nurse.

Ella entered the cottage, astonished to see Jimmy sitting up in bed, rosy cheeked.

"Look at me, Miss. Right as rain, I am. Ye don't need to be frettin' over me."

"But your leg," Ella protested "I need to make sure you are well."

"Nonsense!" Nurse mumbled, and Jimmy waved his arms, swinging them wildly:

"That cloth you put on it did just the trick! Besides, if I need any help, I will just ask Nurse!"

"You need to finish what you started, Dear," smiled Nurse, and she nodded at the door.

Ella heard the sound of the birds, beckoning. Could she really attend the last night of festivities? She hardly dared hope. She looked at Nurse and recalled wise words spoken during her childhood: *Hope is desire, expectation, and preparation.* She thought about how well that fit, and how much action it required from her. She knew she could do it.

She lifted up her skirts and fairly ran her fastest ever to the grotto, following the flock of doves, leading her to her Dear Mother's grave and the shaking hazel tree.

A soft breeze ran through the grotto and the leaves on the little hazel tree shimmered. Ella heard the flutter of bird's wings and looked around to behold all her winged friends who began to sing of Joy and Sorrow, but mostly of the Promise of Joy.

In the midst of the flocks, the birds parted for the swallows to come forward carrying within their beaks the most spectacular dress ever made. The fabric was soft and floated down into Ella's hands.

Golden threads with traces of silver sparkled in the night. Its substance suggested star magic. Overlays of gossamer silk made it better than the finest silk from the furthest lands, and it flowed from finger to finger as she let it play between her fingers. It flowed like water in cloth form.

It shimmered and glowed from the off-the-shoulder neckline, to the empire waist to the tips of the hem. Hammered gold formed the bodice and trimmed the hem, visible under the gossamer layers.

Eleanor smiled as she slipped it on.

Meanwhile the calandra larks brought her a pair of glass slippers with gold trim that fit perfectly on her feet. As she slipped her feet into the glass slippers, her hair fell from it's braid, and hung in its natural length, long and lustrous down her back.

Ella was speechless as she accepted the gifts and whispered thank yous as she walked from the grotto, in through the side door and out to see if Thomas had the carriage. Sure enough, Thomas was waiting with the spare carriage, and they were off to the festival!

As soon as Ella entered the hall, a hush took hold of the crowd. The dress's curves moved with her figure and accentuated the metallic accents with the lights in the hall playing on its golden threads and adornments. Ella glimpsed Stepmother and the Stepsisters gaping at her, and then turn, seething mad as she passed them. She glanced at her father, who was with the other men. He set his glass down and stared at her intently.

The whispers and conjectures about the Beautiful Mystery Woman began anew as Ella moved comfortably and freely through the crowd.

The prince was waiting for her to arrive, so he quickly scooped her up from amongst the crowd and onto the dance floor, the moment he spied her. Ella giggled as they began to dance, weaving in and out of the crowd, murmuring in each other's ears sweet nothings that meant everything to each.

"You look amazing tonight," avowed Christophe, glancing deeply into her eyes.

"Not as valiant as you my lord," replied Ella, her eyes twinkling.

"Only your beauty can trump my bravery, my lady," he said as they spun around and joined hands once again.

"Surely you jest my lord, look at all the others!" sighed Ella, briefly glancing at the other young women tapping their feet, waiting to get a chance with the prince.

"They don't have what you have," affirmed the prince in a final tone.

"What is that?" said Ella, looking back at Christophe. The prince smiled broadly as they began the next dance.

When the ball began to simmer down, Ella made as if to leave. Her heart fluttered when she left Christophe's arms.

"I hope he does not miss me right away," thought Ella as she dashed out the front pavilion. She could hear him calling out to his men at arms to follow her, despite her wishes, but she was too quick. As she made her way down the hill from the castle, she felt one of her slippers become loose from the dew that had begun to form.

"No!" She thought as she tried to push it back on while still running down the hill. "I do NOT have time to stop!"

The slipper slipped off, but Ella knew if she stopped that she would be caught, so she continued to run; grabbing her other slipper in her hand and flying towards Thomas and the cart. Meanwhile, one of the servants sent to follow her retrieved the glass slipper, and handed it to the prince. It twinkled in the torchlight as he examined its petite form and beautiful craftsmanship.

Christophe peered at its beauty as an example of his lost love: its perfect figure and form, the excellent craftsmanship of the golden flakes placed perfectly in its structure.

The clock struck midnight.

"Perfect," he thought, as he gripped the slipper tightly and held it against his chest, thinking to feel his mystery woman's heart beating. He somehow knew the slipper would lead him to her.

The Glass Slipper

The next day the prince presented the glass slipper to his father: "Father, may I please find the wearer of this delicate shoe so that she can become my bride?" The king agreed.

With a nod from the king, the prince set out on his journey to find his elusive fair maiden and future bride.
Prince Christophe traveled with an impressive entourage. First, he ventured into town, looking at each shop and cottage. Then he and his retainers stopped in the town square. The royal herald stepped onto the platform next to

the fountain. A young page dressed in royal livery blew on a silver horn and the Herald announced:

Hear ye, Hear ye
Captivated by beauty; committed to True Love,
Prince Christophe comes this day in search of his Bride.
He requests that all young ladies of the Kingdom try on this Glass Slipper to identify his True Lady Love.

Immediately, the town became a bustling center of activity as families hurried to prepare their daughters to present to the Prince.

The herald blew his silver horn and one of His Royal Highness' pages knocked on the door to the Bakers' Store. The herald announced:

Hear ye, Hear ye
Captivated by beauty; committed to True Love,
Prince Christophe comes this day in search of his Bride.
He bids you open your door and present your daughters to try on the Glass Slipper in order to discover his True Lady Love.

The Baker opened the door wiping his hands on his large white apron, and bowed long and low. The Baker's Wife stood to the side to push forward their timid daughter who was much too short to be the mystery woman. The daughter was vaguely covered in a fine dusting of flour.

The Prince's steward brought forth a velvet-covered stool with the Prince's emblem embroidered on the seat. He produced a little brush to wipe the stool perfectly clean, and then with a flourish indicated that the Baker's Daughter should have a seat. A page carried the Glass Slipper forward on a matching velvet pillow.

Prince Christophe said:

"I have lost my fair maiden three times on three successive nights, and now I will find her by this symbolic yet very real action. If your foot fits this glass slipper, then you shall be my True Love and future queen."

The steward proceeded to take the Glass Slipper and try it on the foot of the Baker's Daughter. She lifted her skirts and the steward slipped the beautiful shoe underneath and around her foot. As soon as he let go, however, the shoe fell off! Her foot was much to small to even contemplate the slipper as hers.

"Thank you for your patience, mademoiselle," said the Prince. The entourage moved to the next dwelling.

The herald again blew his silver horn and one of His Royal Highness' pages knocked on the door to the Butcher's Store. The herald announced:

> *Hear ye, Hear ye*
> *Captivated by beauty; committed to True Love,*
> *Prince Christophe comes this day in search of his Bride.*
> *He bids you open your door and present your daughters to try on the Glass Slipper in order to discover his True Lady Love.*

The Butcher opened the door and stood with his legs spread wide and his hands on his hips. He was so big, his frame fit the entire doorway. Four little girls peeked out from around his legs.

The Prince's steward brought forth the velvet-covered stool with the Prince's emblem embroidered on the seat, along with the little brush to wipe it clean. Then with a flourish he asked if any of the Butcher's daughters were old enough to attend the festival. Alas they were many years to young, so the entourage moved on.

The herald blew his silver horn once again, and one of His Royal Highness' pages knocked on the door to the Weaver's Cottage.[75] The herald announced:

> *Hear ye, Hear ye*
> *Captivated by beauty; committed to True Love,*
> *Prince Christophe comes this day in search of his Bride.*
> *He bids you open your door and present your daughters to try on the Glass Slipper in order to discover his True Lady Love.*

The Weaver opened the door wiping his hands on his large white apron, and bowed long and low. The Weaver's wife stood to the side while she hugged her daughter before pushing her out the door.

The Prince's steward brought forth the velvet-covered stool with the Prince's emblem embroidered on the seat, and he also produced the little brush to wipe it clean. With a flourish, he indicated that the Weaver's Daughter should have a seat. The Glass Slipper was brought forward on a matching velvet pillow.

Prince Christophe said:

> *"I have lost my fair maiden three times on three successive nights, and now I will find her by this symbolic yet very real action. If your foot fits this glass slipper, then you shall be my True Love and future queen."*

The steward proceeded to take the Glass Slipper and try it on the foot of the Weaver's daughter. She lifted her skirts and the steward slipped the beautiful shoe underneath and around her foot.[76] As soon as he let go, however, her foot was so large, that the precious slipper did not fit one toe--much less her foot, and it fell to the ground! The girl kept trying to push in her foot, such that her face turned reddish-purple with the effort, and the Prince called a halt, lest the Glass Slipper shatter.

"Thank you for your patience, mademoiselle," said the Prince. The entourage moved to the next dwelling and the next. They continued to knock on doors until it was dark, with no success that day.

The Prince and his men started again the next day and the next, working all week until they had visited every dwelling in the village. Wondering what was next and just before the day was out, the prince gazed upon a man who was leading a magnificent stallion and two stable boys through the center of the village. On the saddle of the impressive horse were two large fabric boxes of a deep green and a metallic gold.

"My lord!" called the prince to the man "Come here please." The man turned around and walked to the prince, but quickly got on his knee and formally addressed him:

"Your Highness, I apologize that I did not recognize you more quickly!"

"You are forgiven, but I am curious," replied the prince. "What plans do you have for this material?"

"Your Highness," replied the man, "My two beautiful daughters requested this material."

"I confess, that is what I wondered. Could you take me to your daughters?" requested the prince.

"Of course" said the man, gesturing to a stable boy.

"Thomas, please send one of these boys ahead to alert the house of His Highness, Prince Christophe's arrival." Jimmy immediately jumped up on his grey horse and galloped away, while Father led Prince Christophe and his entourage to the chateau. Immediately upon hearing of the Prince's imminent arrival, the Stepsisters rushed to their rooms to prepare for his presence. They cast off their dresses, undoing their hair. Screamed commands ensued from both rooms as the finest of their dresses were demanded. Chambermaids and heaps of apparel alike flew from the room as each stepsister tried to pick the very best dress in order to impress the prince. Maids plastered their hair to their heads without a strand out of place. Their nails were quickly polished in Ella's apricot glaze, and accented with jewelry sparkling in the lamplight.

Upon arrival, the royal herald blew his horn and one of His Royal Highness' pages gave notice to the footman at the front doors. Instantly, Stepmother and the Stepsisters appeared on the threshold. The herald announced:

Hear ye, Hear ye
Captivated by beauty; committed to True Love,
Prince Christophe comes this day in search of his Bride.
He bids you open your door and present your daughters to try on the Glass Slipper in order to discover his True Lady Love.

Galiena pushed her way forward, and said, "I am the eldest, and I am sure you will be more than pleased to discover the slipper is mine, Dearest Christophe."

The Prince's steward brought forth the velvet-covered stool with the Prince's emblem embroidered on the seat, pulled out the little brush to wipe it clean. With a flourish he indicated that Galiena should have a seat, but she was already there! The Glass Slipper was brought forward on a matching velvet pillow.

Prince Christophe said:

> *"I have lost my fair maiden three times on three successive nights, and now I will find her by this symbolic yet very real action. If your foot fits this glass slipper, then you shall be my True Love and future queen."*

The steward proceeded to reach for the Glass Slipper, but Galiena quickly picked up the shoe from off the velvet pillow and held it in her hands, examining its beauty and sparkling golden leaves within the glass. She placed it under her skirts herself, and tried to force her foot into it. After several unsuccessful attempts, she looked around at those assembled, and claimed that she needed to remove an article of clothing before she could truly try on the slipper. She took a deep breath, stood up, and walked over to one of the benches pushed against the wall of the entrance to the manor.

Galiena tried to force the shoe on again, but it would not budge. No amount of force would allow her foot to slide into the shoe. She laughed, almost like a hiccup, after several attempts, and her mother approached her with her back turned to the Prince. She ushered Galiena inside the chateau, and the entire entourage followed.

"Good thing you have such pretty feet!" declared Stepmother, guiding Galiena to a tall-back chair while simultaneously reaching down to try and help her daughter force the slipper. Stepmother gestured to the girl's toes, which were far too large to fit into the slipper, and made a slight motion towards them.

"Cut off your toe" whispered Stepmother without moving her lips. "When you are queen, you will have no need for walking." She handed her a knife while she distracted the prince and his attendants.

Stepmother straightened herself and approached the prince, "So now that you have found your mystery woman," she said clearing her throat, "what are your plans?"

Galiena grimaced as she cut off the toe in one swift motion. She stood up as she pushed her foot into the slipper, thankful for the smooth golden sole that allowed her bleeding toe to slide in easily and well.

"Your Highness," Galiena said as she stood and curtsied, "The shoe fits"

The prince smiled and scooped her up into his arms. "Darling!" he exclaimed, and walked outside. "Our carriage awaits." He handed her inside the carriage, and as he stepped up to join her, he thought he heard voices from up, near the eaves.

"Oh my, look at all that blood!" said the first voice in a singsong voice tone.

"Oh my, that must have hurt," sang the second voice.

Prince Christophe looked around, but only saw two white doves perched near a window. He continued mounting the carriage, and sat next to Galiena. He looked around to make sure all was secure, and as he did, he saw blood seeping from out of the glass slipper.

"What is this?" he cried.

He calmly helped Galiena out of the carriage and allowed her to walk back into the house before following. He called for a bucket of water so the blood could be washed off her foot and off the slipper.

"Thank you for your er . . . diligence, mademoiselle," said the Prince. "Is there another sister?" he asked the family.

Isana, immediately sat in the chair Galiena had so recently vacated.

"I am so sorry for my sister's deception your Highness. I did not know what to do. She is older you know, and I just could not bear to stand and wait a minute longer, but I knew it would end poorly and it did you see, and oh, oh my!" Isana found a similar problem to her sister's dilemma previously. The shoe was too tight, and she squeezed her toes in, but she could not lower her heel.

Once again, her mother came to the rescue with a knife. "Here you are, Isana. Take this knife and cut off your heel and I will distract the prince. Isana did as she was bid as her mother distracted the prince and his attendants, and then quickly slipped her foot into the shoe.

Despite the pain of her heel, Isana stood and then curtsied to the Prince "There you see, all is well, and I am ready to go with you."

The prince smiled and scooped her up into his arms. "Darling!" he exclaimed, and walked outside. "Our carriage awaits."

The prince looked at the shoe, saw no blood, and scooped her up and took her to the carriage. He placed her gently onto the seat and walked around to take his when he heard from above his head.

"Oh, so much blood!" said one, "That shoe is too small!" said another. The prince looked up, confused, but only saw two doves cooing at one another.

Out of curiosity, the prince looked at the shoe on Isana's feet and noticed it now pooling with blood: "Such a disappointment," he said as he stood up and climbed down from the carriage. He offered her his hand and helped her back inside.

"Thank you for your desires, mademoiselle," said the Prince. He called once again for a bucket of water.

Ella had been watching from a corner of the hall, just out of sight. After hearing all the commotion and seeing the royal livery outside in the drive, she had slowly crept up the hall to where she could see her True Love, Prince Christophe. Her heart fluttered when he spoke. Her eyes followed his every movement, even though her body was frozen still, lest she be caught out of her room or the kitchens.

His Royal Highness turned to Father and asked "Is there no other daughter in your home?"

My youngest Daughter Eleanor is lovely, but she was not at the festival, Your Highness.," submitted Father.

"My lord, she cannot possibly be the one. She has been here al…" said Stepmother.

"Please bring her to me now," bluntly interrupted the Prince.

Eleanor came forward. Prince Christophe's heart stirred, but he hardly dared hope. Ella glanced at the Prince, and then around the room. She dropped into a curtsy.

"Good afternoon, Your Highness."

Prince Christophe nodded at the herald who announced:

> *Hear ye, Hear ye*
> *Captivated by beauty; committed to True Love,*
> *Prince Christophe comes this day in search of his Bride.*
> *He bids you present your daughter to try on the Glass Slipper in order to find his True Lady Love.*

Eleanor arranged her skirts gently around her ankles as she sat on the stool and smiled at the steward as he knelt before her. He held the velvet cushion with the glass slipper in his hands. Her heart pounded as she felt the Prince's gaze, intent on her face combined with the memories of all three nights. She knew what was about to happen, and she wanted to savor every moment. She felt her heart pounding, and beheld her True Love standing before her with his heart in his eyes, yet he knew her not. . . or did he?

Prince Christophe said:

> *"I have lost my fair maiden three times on three successive nights, and now I will find her by this symbolic yet very real action. If your foot fits this glass slipper, then you shall be my True Love and future queen."*[77]

The steward proceeded to reach for the Glass Slipper.

Watching the action, Galiena complained, "What is she waiting for? Why does she not just admit that she would never in a thousand years wear a glass slipper and stop wasting our time?"

"My foot huts," whined Isana.

"Hush!" hissed Stepmother.

Father simply stood and watched. The steward took the slipper and extended it just under the hem of her dress, and everyone rubbed their eyes, for it seemed that a sliver of silver stars shimmered out from around the shoe as it disappeared under Eleanor's dress. She stood up and stepped forward with the slipper on her foot. She spun around on the one-slippered foot, and Prince Christophe caught her in his arms and held her tight, close to his chest. He looked at her deeply, drinking in the depth of her eyes, and knew without a doubt, that he had found his mystery woman, his True Love.

"My beautiful Mystery Woman! It is you: My True Love,[78] just as you said, here in my own lands, waiting for me to find you. Will you tell me your name, My Lady?"

"Yes I will, My Prince. My name is Ella....Eleanor."

"You are beautiful, Eleanor. Will you marry me?" He went down on one knee.

"Yes I will, Christophe."

Prince Christophe smiled broadly, and his eyes lit as if with fire. Ella wiped tears from her eyes. He jumped up with glee, scooped her off the floor, and carried her not to the carriage, but to his snowy white horse, Flurry. Christophe set Ella gently atop Flurry, and set off to the castle at a slow walk. As they passed the town, the people cheered. They spoke of their feelings of being apart from each other, of the long sleepless nights, of the fluttering in their stomachs that reminded them of each other. There was a soft singing in the air as they reached the castle, and Ella realized her avian friends had joined them in jubilation.

Ella and Christophe planned the most beautiful of weddings to be held in the largest pavilion available; its center poles stood far taller than her chateau and many parts of the castle, too. A chandelier was placed in between them to light the immense space underneath. As soon as the pavilion was erected and fully prepared, the altar was placed at the head of the tent with flowers draped about the wooden benches.

Prince Christophe and Princess Eleanor married and lived happily ever after to the end of their days.

The End

What is a Hero Princess?

The Hero Princess is both a concept and a description. She is the champion inside each of us who embraces the idea of engaging the Universal Quest, reaching toward a lifelong Journey that encompasses the Pursuit of Excellence. The goal is to discover and embrace the True, Authentic Self.

In 2009, Dr. Piper Winifred gathered together a group of twelve junior scholars to research the idea of *The Quest.* The task set before the group was to look seriously at theories and outlines designated as *The Hero's Journey*, and chart or compare this trope to classical tales. The research team explored the topic in detail, and within three months chose Fairy Tales as a starting point. ***The Fairy Tale Project*** was born. Our topic, according to tradition and traditional experts, studied story paradigms and archetypal themes. We read centuries' worth of stories from around the world. We drew charts and graphs on several whiteboards. We compiled piles of notes, and felt frustrated because something was missing. It didn't take long for a member of our group to burst out with, "Ok, I get it. We need the Hero Prince, but where is the Hero Princess?!?!" After a long conversation, we began an extensive search for the true partner to the Hero Prince: the Hero Princess. Would we find her?

By the beginning of 2010, we had the parameters in place for our search for the conceptual Hero Princess. We looked to the bold and notable women in History. Would their real life stories match archetypal paradigms? What if we applied similar methods as those that previous experts had employed in studying the tales of great men in history? The results were AMAZING!

This was an innovative experience as no known record reveals this approach by any group of scholars; the universal comparison of literary characters, scriptural models, and archetypal themes to actual, living heroines, and what the life stages and methods for maneuvering through the woman's journey had to be or become for success. Were they similar?

We found the Hero Princess, and tracked her in both History and Story. For two more years we followed her trail. It was FUN (and "Fun" is an understatement)! We were surprised—and not surprised. We were amazed at what we found and where we found her: we found her EVERYWHERE!

Not only did we find her, but we unlocked a paradigm that allows for mapping stories from ancient times to modern day. Why? Because it recognizes both women and men as part of the ongoing story of human existence. It's pretty simple, really. Not only did we find common patterns and themes in looking at the Woman's Journey, but we found common or universal story paradigms and thus, became adept at mapping the story.

The Hero Princess is a necessary and interesting piece of the human story throughout time. Her role is as varied as there are women. The female hero is archetypal just like the male hero. She is YOU and she is ME. Her story and THE story cannot be taken away from what is life and where we come from. The Male story, or the so-called Hero's Journey does not exist without the Female story and the Heroine's Journey. The journeys are different, but they co-exist.

We decided to call both male and female Hero, because the differences are not so much about gender as they are about the underpinnings of society and a Hero is a Champion and what value a Champion holds for a society.

Once we peel back the layers of the last few centuries and uncover the authentic versions of the stories handed down over generations of time, we discover true wisdom. Practical wisdom that reads like "truth" has been embedded in tales since the beginning of time.

The first step for any individual is identifying our Archetype. The second step encompasses understanding it, in order to recognize our representative self in stories through mapping the story. At that point, we are ready to Quest. As we Chart our Path, we find a wealth of resources available, having been passed down through the ages via the Practical Wisdom embedded in stories.

To learn more, please visit: www.theHeroPrincess.com

Path ~ Journey ~ Quest

The Heroine's Journey is about knowing who you are, finding your source of power, and following your Path for the benefit of the story you create in life.

What is a Path?

Each of us creates our Path every day.
The Path = Movement in Life through Time.

Seven processes form each of our individual paths. We are individuals who

1. think,
2. feel,
3. believe,
4. imagine,
5. act,
6. connect, and
7. reflect.

As we move forward in our lives –or as we exist within time-- the interaction of those seven processes determines the shape and direction of our Path.

What is a JOURNEY?

As discovered through the ages through Wonder Tales, Epic Stories, Fairy and Folk Tales, there are 7 Keys to a Woman's Path. This is a Universal Construct. Each of these 7 Keys is essential, and represents progress on a Personal Journey. We can think of the keys As opening doorways to paths on Your Personal Journey.
A key opens a door to a Path. The combination of these paths becomes Your Journey.

The 7 Keys for the Journey

These are universal constructs, and each is essential for wholeness in life:

- *Meaningful Happiness*
- *Friendship Factors*
- *Confidence Ratio*
- *Family & Career*
- *Decision Making Processes*
- *Power & Authority*
- *Public vs. Private Balance*

While the 7 Keys open or lead to Paths that are essential, there is another Journey Process that is also important. This is the Heroine's Journey, and it occurs along the way. The Heroine's Journey happens because you are willing to use the keys and each day you once again choose to Journey.

The Steps of the Heroine's Journey:

1. Self
2. Mentor(s)
3. Friends
4. Roles
5. Tradition
6. Liminality
7. Personal Power

•

The phases, or the process that occurs during each of these steps:

1. Loss of Innocence
2. Longing
3. Betrayal
4. In Search of the Mother
5. The Search for the Father
6. Death
7. Belonging

•

These phases or processes are like questions we ask and answer in the form of personal experience, which is why we describe this as a Journey.

The answers to these questions or phases are:

1. Maturity
2. Desire
3. True Friendship
4. Identity & Love of/for the Self
5. Security
6. Grief
7. Purpose & Meaning

What is the Quest?

The Quest encompasses the sequence or combination of Journey questions you as a seeker, in search for your True, Authentic Self. The sooner you become the Subject of your Life's Story, instead of a side trail or a minor player in your own life, the better ad more completely you will understand your Life. The does NOT mean that you make your self the focus of everything you do or say . . . this means that you are entirely away of your Self as the agent on the Path, actively making conscious decisions about your Personal Journey, and thus QUESTING!

The Archetypal Female Role

The Archetype of the Heroine is divided into 12 separate Roles within 4 Categories. The Four Categories are:

- Builders
- Shapers
- Explorers, and
- Managers.

When we talk about these women as people we refer to:

- Queens,
- Princesses,
- Seekers, and
- Leaders.

The 12 Archetypes are:

Builders/Queens: High Queen
Nurturing Queen
Fantasy Queen
Shapers/Princesses: Epic Princess
Romance Princess
Warrior Princess
Explorers/Seekers: Adventurer
Scholar
The Creative
Facilitators/Leaders: Social Facilitator
Sensitive Connector
Community Leader

Cinderella is a Community Leader.

About the Author

Dr. Piper Winifred grew up surrounded by stories and storytellers. Her earliest memories consist of long walks with a Dad who was forever reciting poetry and tales of wonder, and of telling tales passed down through generations that always began with, "Once upon a time, there was a little girl named Piper. . ."

Piper lives in Chicago with her cat, Julie, and works to discover the authentic origins and elements of stories paired with a rigorous program of classical and ancient languages, archival research, exploration in dusty, musty places: along with arduous translation, and exacting theoretical standards, which has led to the joy of Storytelling: a lifelong love. Her hope is that you will enjoy celebrating life seen through very human eyes thinking of your very own precious Life, and engage in the Journey.

Discussion Questions & Notes

What follows are three types of questions/answers that correlate to the page numbers from the story. Some are about historical context. Some help us understand how to read the story, or offer another way to look at them as a way of mapping the story. The rest offer questions posed for DISCUSSION in classrooms, book clubs, for fun, and for reflection. They are meant as a tool for further thought, and as an extension to bring alive this beautiful tales that has lasted for over twelve centuries and exists in every culture and land in the world.

Once these Wonder Tales were told to guide children and adults alike in the way that families and societies traditionally have shaped the answers to difficult and complex questions: via story. Because of this, there is no single "correct" answer to these questions. The way we approach life's questions depends on circumstance, station, gender, age, and personal and communal goals. The messages of these tales are consistent: they are about human beings struggling to find answers and to learn correct ways of living.

---

[1] What does "Once Upon a Time" mean?

Fairy Tales are teaching tales, and told purposely in a space of "no time." This writing device is used to alert the reader or listener that these events happen --and have happened--in any time or place because these are universal, human tales that happen to every man/ woman.

[2] Ella's primary virtues are listed here as 'Beauty" and "Sweetness." What does this tell us abut the epitome of womanhood and what is expected of the ideal female?

[3] The imagery is traditional fairy tale imagery. The woods is that timeless place of wonder from which fairy tale magic emanates. The number 7 is a magic number and thus important. The use of the number 7 tells us we are in the right place for the tale we are about to "hear." The red poppy is the #1 women's flower and has

been since the Age of Myth.

[4] The fairs were miniature cities set up solely for trading at that location. Some were open once a year and some grew to become major cities in their own right. To read more about the fairs, see: http://www.medieval-life-and-times.info/medieval-life/medieval-fairs.html

[5] Fashion plays a large role in this story. Historical context: this places the tale in the 12th ce. When commerce changed radically and goods and services opened up due to the many trading venues that expanded to the East. The way commerce changed altered every aspect of society, which is also what is shown in this story. Do we experience that in modern day? (Cultural and societal changes due to business and economic practices?)

[6] This is a story about Tradition, and the Maiden's Dance is one of the longest held traditions in many and various cultures. When a young woman comes of age (usually at about age 15), she is presented to society by way of ritual (in this case the dance with specific costume norms, dance steps and words to the songs) and celebration (the community festival). This makes for a passage in her life she can mark as definitive and also designates her as ready to take the next step in life: marriage. This marks her as part of the community.

What similar rites of passage do we employ in modern day?

Is it the same for men and women?

[7] Mentioning bees is important, for the change that comes in Cinderella tales has to do with new and growing forms of industry. Changes wreak havoc on tradition, but the changes themselves are seen as inherently good, as evidenced by the imagery of the industry of bees.

[8] The traditional dance or maiden's dance is unique to each area and is part of the culture. The dance has specific steps, words to the song, and is known by all. It is part of the Spring Festival celebration.

[9] Now we have a suggestion that it is virtuous or necessary that Ella be "Ladylike." What does this mean, and do the same practices apply in modern day?

[10] This scene with Cook is important, for it helps us understand why the story is about a young woman who works in the kitchen,

and why this is upside down. What is happening here?

[11] Mapping the story: Cats are very common in fairy tales. They identify by gender. Whereas a tomcat will be a wanderer and a rascal, a female cat is domestic, and a guardian of the hearth. A female cat comforts with her purr, and is geared toward preserving home and family.

It is common for animals to serve as companions in Fairy and Folk Tales. Cats are Adventurers and are companion adventurers. A cat's presence in a story means that this is a tale of traveling. It also means that the tale comes from a region and time when roads and trade were making a significant --and new-- impact on society, and the changes meant new stories--or changes in the stories--had to enter the lexicon in order to reflect the new ideas.

CatStitch is very in tune with the traveling that Father undertakes and personifies the new ideas. Important Note: this does not mean that the cat personifies reality, but rather the idea of what people of the time have of the changes they perceive, through the eyes of a cat who has Nine Lives, and therefore can view these changes and survive them.

Do we as listeners of the tale take the place of CatStitch, or do we imagine ourselves having a companion who is a Cat? That depends on whether or not we are an adventurer, and in the time period when these stories originated, societal roles were more clearly defined, so it was easier for a person to know his/her station in life and thus what to expect.

How do we know if we are an Adventurer?

Friendship and/or companionship with animals is a common theme in Fairy & Folk tales. What does this mean that CatStitch is her constant companion and that birds, too are her friends?

What are the attributes we look for in a friend?

What attributes of Ella attracted the animal companions to her?

How do Stories convey these friendship ideals?

Check this list of Attributes:
http://theheroinesjourney.net/friendship-attributes/_Think about the attributes in your current friends, and those that are needed in companions on Your Personal Journey.

[12] Here is the gist of the tale: traditions are safe and lovely, but things are about to change: we don't know how. Change is inevitable, yet scary. Sometimes change comes with scary packages or alongside unwanted elements (like the Stepmother).

All people are born into conditions that exist previous to their having been born, but affect them nevertheless. What does that mean for us, and how do we interact with the character in the story because of this?

[13] Fathers are often absent in fairy tales. Mapping the story: "The absentee father" is a common theme we want to understand. Why is he gone? First, in history, many fathers have been absent due to wars, crusade, and the general danger of living at this time. As a high profile merchant, Ella's father makes the circuit of fairs along one or more trade routes shown on this map.

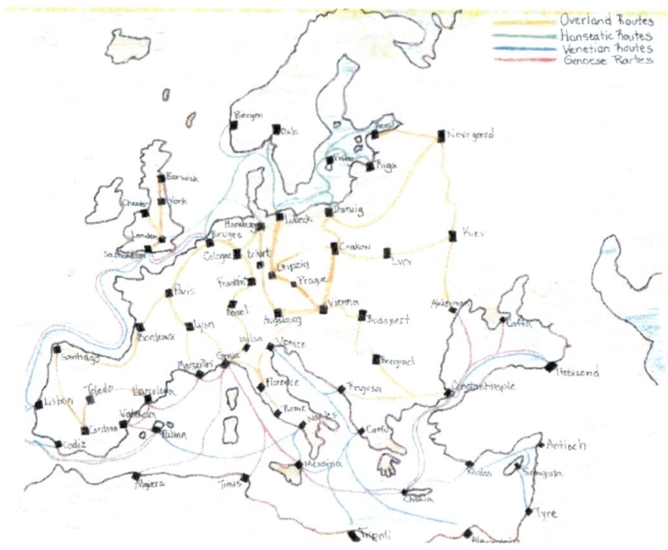

Any given merchant could become very influential in one of the routes depending on his reach and expenditures. How does this compare to commerce today?

[14] How do appearances express a time and persona? What is Ella supposed to look like, and how does that compare to expectations for today's young women?

[15] What is the role of laughter in the story and is it the same as the role of laughter on The Path? Does it fit on one of the Steps of The Path, or all of the Steps of The Path? There is a difference

between characters in the story and their laughter and when the reader is laughing: what is the difference?

[16] Since this is a story about Tradition and Change, take note of the traditions. How many different kinds of traditions are there? Are they sacred and inviolate?
[17] Shampoo is a multi-billion dollar industry. Since the earliest times women have concocted fantastic recipes for pleasure, and for function. We have inherited the recipes along with their lists of ingredients and they remain in our shampoos.

[18] Mapping the Story: One of the primary characters in a fairy tale is the Nurse. The main character must go TO the Nurse in order to find out more about herself and her origins. Unless she takes this step, she will not be able to find her way to freedom or justice, or whatever is her goal.
[19]

[20] Work as Play & Play as preparation is another important element in Story. How does this apply, and can we place it into our lives or the lives of those we love? Why would it be part of a story? How does work—and especially work as play—convey gender roles?

[21] What is happening here? Mother represents the old ways and tradition. She looks ahead at the horizon and sees what is coming. It is inevitable, but she knows that she will not fit in or even belong in the new, coming age. She seems like she is fading away.

[22] Fairy Tale language includes the theme of Maiden, Mother, and Crone. This fits the Rule of Three. It also parallels the three stages of a woman's life and we will always find all three in a fairy tale because the passages to different stages in life is part of the crucial teaching of story. Maiden, Mother, and Crone also refers to the seasons as far as they represent the movement of time.

[23] Arnoldo Fortini, Helen Moak, translator, *Francis of Assisi*, Crossroad Publishing, 1960.

[24] Why are "Fairy Tales" so often about Kings and Queens, Princes and Princesses? Even in the time when Fairy Tales were first told, no such kingdoms as they are portrayed existed except in the imaginations of story-tellers. The castles –or ruins of castles—that we see in different countries did not exist or function as they are portrayed in the tales. What the stories reflect are icons or symbols of archetypal paradigms.

To use *Cinderella* as an example: In our day, the kings of Fairy Tales would more likely be rival industrial leaders or venture capitalists with a great deal of wealth. Their children are privileged, bound to the behaviors of a certain social class, and a part of the world of "power" and control in which they live. The "monsters" represented by the Stepmother and her minions, the Stepsisters are easy to relate to when we think in terms of corrupt government, ruthless business leaders, tyrants, and hidden dangers.

Almost every fairy tale written describes a situation where justice has failed, and a Hero is allowed an opportunity to fix it. Will the Quest be realized? That is always the question, for Injustice has always existed in the world, and it usually takes a valiant and noble heart to face the Quest. THAT is why the Hero is a Prince or Princess: because only a Hero Princess or a Hero Prince qualifies, and THAT is what these stories tell us: if we hear "the Call" of the Quest, then we, too, can be a Hero Princess (or Prince) According to our attributes and nobility of character, just like Ella. The odds are against her, but she practices virtue and rights the wrongs in her world!

[25] When mapping a story, notice anything that mentions numbers, steps, or timing. It is always significant. What role does the hour of midnight play? In this story, it emphasizes the theme, which has to do with Change.

Mapping the story: When we read about the passing of the day in a fairy tale then we interpret what we read as "real." This is interesting and important, because it elevates what could be a "dream sequence" into the strongest reality of the story.

[26] Since this is a Fairy Tale, we know that our heroine has a Quest to complete. How do we know what it is, and more importantly, how does she? At which point has she reached her goal? How do we determine the "task"? Is it a question of a beginning, a middle, and an end?

In our own lives do we have one giant Quest or many little ones and how do we know where we are?

[27] Again we notice an emphasis on fashion and take note. This is a product of changes in tradition and thus style, and it is also a result of the changes in the material world.

[28] What does the Stepmother represent metaphorically? What about the Stepsisters? As the abrupt new era comes directly to Ella's front door and right inside her home and family, what do the changes look like and feel like?

[29] How often do we let a bad situation turn into a worse one

because it encroaches slowly or we fail to stop it in the beginning?

[30] Fallacy of the conquered. This story is full of *post hoc ergo propter hoc* fallacy and this will need to be corrected if Ella is to take control of her life. How will this happen and what will it look like?

[31] Is Ella a child? How does this work for her or against her? Is this part of the Maiden, Mother, Crone construct at work? Have you been in this position?

[32] Notice that she speaks as if it is a done deed, and it is. Not only is Mother gone, but also the memory of the mother is gone. Now everyone needs to catch up.

[33] Ella solves her dilemmas by going to work, often doing the job or task of a servant. She does not order a servant to do it or give up because the task would not be her role. No one comes and solves her problems for her except that she does something first. Thinking about how Fairy and Folk Tales are teaching tales, what does this teach? (Considering what is being taught.) Is this also about gender roles?

[34] Upheaval and change trickles down throughout an entire society or community.

Ella's community is suffering. Do we sometimes make choices in a different way when our friends or loved ones are involved than when it is only our own discomfort? Is this a good thing or a bad thing?

[35] The Hero's Quest vs. the Heroine's Quest is an important topic for consideration. One of the reasons for this is the meeting of friends and companions or helpers is a different part of the Quest for women than for men.

This is one of the most important ways that Fairy and Folk Tales teach: by demonstrating everyday, ordinary actions that are part of correct behavior for human beings who live together. Do modern stories show this same process of values and attributes?

[36] In our time, would we like our leaders or the elite members of society to recognize and be aware of the mundane, everyday realities of life?

[37] For what is this a metaphor?

[38] What do you think about her apology here? Should she say "I'm sorry…" How often do we do this? Is there a better alternative?

[39] What do you think about the Stepmother? Is she a monster? What about the Stepsisters?

[40] What is service?

[41] Bread is the staff of life. Why is this important?

[42] Good guys live in communities. Bad guys live in isolation. Stepmother repeatedly reveals that she does not understand the idea of community even though it is all around her. She also refuses to do her part or play her role in the community, even when it would be easy.

Stepmother plays the role of the Monster because she is an enemy to humans, and has no feeling for the sanctity of human life. The Stepsisters are Minions. Their extreme self-centeredness is the clue.

Ella wins her battle against the Stepmother by not engaging her in a battle. How does that work? Is this another instance of the Heroine's Journey being different from the Hero's Journey?

What do these symbolic story elements mean in this story, and more importantly, can we find corollaries in our own lives? How do we notice it?

[43] Stepmother is more concerned with the style of Ella's hair than whether or not the people on her properties have food to eat. What does this show and is this a common indicator of changing times? What does it reveal?

[44] What does it mean to be useful? Is it enough to just be?

[45] The idea of "sacred tears" or "holy weeping" has a long pedigree in a wide variety of cultures. Water gives life and Holy Water can bestow life.

[46] Mapping the Story: Gifts in Story are important. In Romance tales gifts alert us to the presence of a change in the path. In Epic tales, gifts alert us to the presence of tradition at work. In a Fairy or Folk Tale, a gift is a signal that Destiny has just intervened. The gift is a Consequence, and will lead to Opportunity.

[47] What does each girl essentially ask for and what is the metaphor? What would you ask for?

[48] A merchant gains power, not through money, but through influence.

[49] Hazel Tree is associated with magic and water. The greatest significance is transformation of life, the self, and one's surroundings. Making a wish while holding hazelnut branch or twig or tree means one's wishes will come true

[50] Is it possible to show gratitude towards a monster? Put another way: is it possible to show gratitude towards an entity that does not recognize it?

[51] Father questions the changes but does not wonder about them. Why is that?

[52] Fairy Tales did not originally refer to fairies or even a mythical fairyland, but rather to the word "Faerie" which works back to the word "Fata," or Fate. This tale has no fairies, although we encounter a mystical element in Eleanor's ability to talk to animals (common in Fairy Tales) and in her link to her Dear Mother, who is dead, but maybe not all the way? Since her mother represents "Tradition" this is a working metaphor and not supernatural or a fairy. The story is a reflection of fate or destiny.. The heroine, the hero (a supporting actor) and their companions do not "cause" the Dark Fate, but rather inherit it. Is this one way to explain the darkness in the world, and is it realistic?

[53] What is Ella's talent? How does it work? How do we gain strength and power from our environment, and can we keep it?

Mapping the Story: In a story about Tradition and Change, Ella has changed her environment by placing the hazel twig on her mother's grave, thus setting a scenario for her new Path. Is it possible for us to practice this in our dealings with monsters and other obstacles?

Up until the 19th century, Nature was considered an active part of God and religion, including in the Christian religion. It is only in the modern age that Nature became a part of the scientific realm. This is why we see nature as an active part of Fairy Tales, and thus, see it as operating on the side of "Good."

Before the 11th century, the roots of "Cinderella" did not lie in Fairy or Folk tales, but rather in Saga, which were heavily laces with nature as an active element in the story.

[54] Linden flower tea promotes good health and is extremely calming.

[55] Context: being part of the community is important and Ella's

father is the merchant involved in textiles. Here, she is sitting with Nurse who is involved in weaving, but it is not that simple. The sheep must be sheared, and the wool carted or corded, and then washed, dyed and spun. Before that there is work to be done too because the flock of sheep are guarded by a shepherd and his dog. Once the fabric is woven and sold by a merchant, someone like Mrs. Henderson will stitch it together. Each person in a community does their part, and Ella fits in.

A significant aspect of placing Ella into the community via story is that the listener of the tale remembers where the wool (and thus the cloth) comes from. We each need to remember where our tools and resources come from and where we came from in order to arrive at where we are going.

[56] Mapping the story: In fairy tales, birds are connections to heaven and serve as messengers. They are "good,"

[57] Ella walks back and forth to the Grotto. This appears to be an important Path in this tale. How long is a Path and what is a Journey? Can important paths be hidden and then appear through Mindfulness?

See http://theimaginedfuture/
to understand the nature of *The Path* in Story.

Mapping the Story: Is it a True Path if we do not choose it our self, but rather, it is chosen for us? To decide, see to:

[58] What do you think about Stepmother's inability to notice the origin of the beautiful songs or see the songbirds, or even recognize what she is hearing? Is this a negation of beauty, of Nature? Is she clueless or deceiving herself?

Do we see this behavior in modern day?

[59] What do you think about the Avian Symphony? Has a song or music ever helped you in a crucial situation or time? Why is that? In Mapping the Story, what does the song tell us? To what element(s) is it linked?

[60] Allowing memory to have a voice is an important part of the grieving process.

[61] If the dresses have been burned, and now only exist in the memories, is the tradition gone?

[62] Gratitude is the key ingredient for Happiness. How is gratitude manifested in Ella's life, and how is it manifested in your own?

[63] What kind of monster is Stepmother? For information on the Monster Path and monster motivations see:
http://discoveryourarchetype
Also see detailed descriptions of types within the monster categories.

[64] *Baw me bairne, sleep softly now.* The tune is also known as *Blue Eyed Ennis.*

[65] The "awful task" is a common element of Fairy and Folk Tales. It is an essential element of The Quest. Just as in this story, it doesn't make much sense in its particulars, for it is symbolic. The ridiculous nature of the chores that Stepmother has Ella undertake leaves us baffled, but that is part of the point: it is a learning point and it is not about the chores. It also is not supposed to make sense to human beings (what monsters do). This represents Eleanor's Quest, and she will necessarily need to embark on a Journey or a series of Journeys to complete her Quest.
Journey: http://theimaginedfuture.com
Quest:
http://theimaginedfuture.com
[66] This moment lies in juxtaposition of the previous reflections of Joy and Sorrow.

[67] What is a relationship, and how do stories pass on the characteristics and elements? How are manners conveyed? Do specific relationships require a name and is this how we identify them throughout our lives?

What is a companionship, and how is it different from other relationships? Why do we need to know, and how do stories teach this? Why has this element faded over time, and has it had any effect on society?

Relationships are one of--if not THE--most powerful resources known to humankind throughout the ages. History and Story tell us so.

[68] See; http://www.thefinertimes.com/Middle-Ages/dance-in-the-middle-ages.html

[69] What makes tradition? Where does it Come from? It is more

than just repetition and more than Time.

What are your traditions, and what is the difference between

- Personal traditions
- Familial traditions
- Community traditions
- Religious traditions

Are they always seen as traditions, or are they sometimes known by other names or categories?

[70] What is ordinary? Is it possible that uniqueness is discovered once we get to know someone, so all that is required is being ourselves?

[71] Historical context: This story comes from a time when 'royalty' was still forming and knights and other warriors became kings, but needed to choose their brides from among "the best" families. Often, the so-called aristocratic families had the wealth due to engaging in commerce or city affairs that the warrior class appointed to royalty needed. This does not mean that royalty married commoners, but it does show a loosening along hierarchical boundaries during times of change.

[72] Three is a magic number in fairy tales. If it exists in a companionship or grouping, then it means completeness. If it exists as a comparison, then it is the formula: too much/too big; too little/too small/not enough; just right. If it is about timing then it is similar to the formula: get ready, get set, GO! And we know that it is/was recognizable as such in its time and place.

[73] How do you negotiate time to rest? Is rest part of The Path? What step is it and how do we know?

[74] One of the attributes of a True Hero is the willingness to make a sacrifice. Ella wants to go to the festival, but she does not hesitate in staying to care for Jimmy.

[75] The Rule of Three operates at a more complex level here as we see the Prince visit three separate households to demonstrate completeness. This tells us that he visited ALL the houses and shops.

[76] The metaphor of the Glass Slipper is tremendous and well known. What can we say about "If the shoe fits"? Can we also ask, "If the shoe does not fit"?

---

[77] In traditional stories, when anything is repeated, it means that it is important and is meant to be an important lesson. Often, it is a takeaway lesson, or in other words, it is not even necessary to the story, but a separate teaching element. This is not the same as a Fable, where there is a one-line teaching lesson. The lessons of Wonder Tales are more complex and dynamic. What is the takeaway lesson in this segment of the story?

[78] What is True Love? Does it have something to do with the Glass Slipper? (Keep in mind that the Prince did not provide the Slipper.) Is it about an ideal, or was the ideal configured by the couple themselves during the festival? How do we know? What does "True" mean?

What questions remain?

Made in the USA
Monee, IL
18 June 2025

19192421R00067